AFTER THE
Vows

USA TODAY BESTSELLING AUTHOR
CLAUDIA BURGOA

www.claudiayburgoa.com

Also By Claudia Burgoa

Be sure to sign up for my newsletter where you'll receive news about upcoming releases, sneak previous, and also FREE books from other bestselling authors.

After the Vows is also available in Audio

The Way of Us

Meant For Me

Finally Found You

Where We Belong

Luna Harbor

Finally You

Perfectly You

Always You

Truly You

Against All Odds: The St. James Family

Until Next Time, Love

Something Like Love

Betting on Love

Accidentally in Love

Waiting for Love

Decker Family Novels

Unexpected Everlasting:

Suddenly Broken

Suddenly Us

Somehow Everlasting:

Love Like Her

Second Chance Sinners Duet
Pieces of Us
Somehow Finding Us

My One
My One Regret
My One Desire

The Everhart Brothers

Fall for Me
Fight for Me
Perfect for Me
Forever with Me

Mile High Billionaires
Finding My Reason
Something Like Hate
Someday, Somehow

Standalones

Chasing Fireflies
Until I Fall
Christmas in Kentbury

Chaotic Love Duet

Begin with You

Back to You

Co-writing

Holiday with You

Home with You

Here with You

Dear Reader,

I write highly emotional romances that include thought provoking subjects. If you would like to see a list of them, please check the link below with more information.

This book has a cliffhanger, it's necessary to read Who We Love to fulfill the most anticipated HEA.

TW Website

Happy Reading,
Claudia

For my personal Seth—
for supporting me while I get lost in my world,
and make sure to take care of me and the family

"Instead of saying, "I'm damaged, I'm broken, I have trust issues" say "I'm healing, I'm rediscovering myself, I'm starting over."

— Horacio Jones

Prologue

Seth

SOME THINGS ARE UNFORGETTABLE.

They stick around in the place where they happened—even when our minds bury them deep in the darkness, they still exist.

Some others… no matter what we do, never disappear. The images come back during the night, haunting us like a bad scene from *Friday the 13th*.

It's been almost eight years.

Eight long, painful years.

Many would think it's over.

That we had all forgotten and moved on.

But it seems like I'm not the only one who still remembers.

Of course, I didn't know that until the nightmares became real, and I had to run for my life. All the training I received from a young age to become an agent for the secret, high-security intelligence company Dad owns isn't enough to stay alive.

Eight years ago, when the mission didn't go as we expected, we returned and took care of the cartel. We erased all evidence of our existence. However, it seems like someone was left behind—someone who remembers well and wants to play *the last man standing.*

He's wrong about one thing. This isn't a game. It's very real, and they made the fatal mistake of touching the most important person to me.

They might think they're hunting me, but...

They don't know Seth Bradley, do they?

Chapter One

Seth

"WHAT'S ON YOUR MIND?" Mom's green eyes study me the same way she's done ever since I can remember. Nothing gets past her.

Dad should hire her to work with The Organization. She'd be great during interrogations, which is what she does with me half the time. One day, I'll be able to get away with murder, and she won't notice. Can today be that day? The corner of my lip lifts slightly before I shake my head.

"Seth?" My name comes out like a command. It almost sounds like, tell-me-now-or-else.

Ainsley Decker-Bradley is a total boss. Even Dad, a man with hundreds of trained badass agents under his command, does what she says.

Mom crosses her arms, giving me *the look*. The one that says, don't-make-me-ask-again.

My shoulders slump in resignation. "Why does your husband have to summon me at six in the fucking morning? It's…"

I toss my hands up in the air. I'm annoyed because I don't know how to finish the sentence. She's going to defend my father. She always has some excuse for why he behaves the way he does. I guess that's why he loves her so much.

"Never mind."

She rolls her eyes. "You remind me so much of him when he was younger."

"Him? As in, Dad?" I chuckle. "You're wrong. That would be Nathan. He's the one almost exactly like your husband."

I don't add that Grace, my older sister—and their miracle baby—is just like her.

Me? I'm… Who am I in this dynamic?

I'm too young to compare with Princess Grace and too old to catch a break like our youngest brother. To top it all off, I have to compete with a ghost who never existed—James.

Mom walks toward me, cups my cheek with one hand, and says, "I wish you wouldn't be so hard on yourself and your father."

I don't understand what that means, and before I can ask,

Dad waltzes into the kitchen. He's carrying his tablet. "Morning, Nine." He brushes his lips against Mom's, calling her the same ridiculous nickname he's had for her since they were young.

The next thing I know he's placing his tablet on the counter, hugging my mother and dipping her as if this was an old romantic movie. It takes all my effort not to roll my eyes and leave the kitchen. They can be disgusting in the morning... and the afternoon. It's like they haven't outgrown the honeymoon stage of their relationship, and they've been together for over thirty-five years.

I clear my throat. "Mind taking this to your room?"

Dad releases Mom from the embrace and glares at me. I'd love to ask him what the fuck I did now, but I plaster a fake smile on my face and wait for my father to chide me.

He grabs his tablet, unlocks it, and hands it to me. "I can't keep using my resources to erase your digital print every single day of the week. 'Rumor has it that Coco LeBlanc's relationship with Seth Bradley'"—he glares at me—"*grandson of Gabe Colt and Chris Decker*, is heading to the altar. They were spotted outside Tiffany's in New York—'"

"Are you keeping track of me?" I interrupt him, instead of pulling out my phone and calling Coco because what the fuck?

She took that picture right before I lectured her about the "harmless little bits of information" she's been posting about me on her social media. That's exactly what she called them, harmless. It doesn't matter how often I explain that I don't like it when she shares my image or name. She just doesn't listen to me.

"As you know, we have a department assigned to keep track of my agents so they don't jeopardize The Organization." He takes the tablet away, swiping and tapping a few times. There's a document with links. "There are at least twenty articles about you, Range Communications & Consulting, and the size of the ring you'll be buying her. You need to control this—and rethink this association. Rethink your priorities and stop being so irresponsible."

He says it like Coco doesn't matter, and she's easy to disregard. The dismissiveness is what angers me.

Does he think I don't care about The Organization and the agents? I understand the implications of her indiscretions. I don't like that Range Communications & Consulting—the company I co-own with my best friend—is on the map for all the wrong things. Still, I'm not going to agree with him.

"My relationship with Coco is none of your business," I say defensively.

"It is when you're putting the entire family in jeopardy." His voice booms throughout the entire kitchen.

"You're exaggerating."

Okay, I'm being obtuse and a brat. He's right, but I'm not going to tell him that. If there's one thing I've learned about my father, it's that once I admit he's right, he treats me like a child who needs to learn a lesson. This is beyond my control. My girlfriend has trouble with boundaries. We're working on that.

"Is she worth it?" His question startles me.

"What?" I can't hide the confusion in my voice.

He tilts his head toward Mom. "Do you love this Coco

enough to put your mother in jeopardy? You might as well start painting a target on each of us while you're at it."

Dad knows me too well. He mentions Mom, knowing I adore her and would never let anything happen to her. Yet, he thinks I don't give a shit, but he's wrong. Knowing him, it's pointless to explain that this is out of my control. Unlike him, I understand that people have free will and we can't restrain them all the time.

Will I have a long discussion with Coco about this?

Yes.

I rub my temples, mentally preparing for what's going to be a long, loud fight with the woman everyone knows as my girlfriend.

Is she worth going through all this trouble?

Well, that's a different issue that I don't discuss with anyone, and honestly, I don't want to deal with it now, and maybe not ever.

We're convenient.

She has a steady relationship, as her PR company required when they asked me to take on the role. It was a favor to Aunt Pria, but it also became a favor to me.

What do I get in exchange? I can keep my thoughts and dick away from the forbidden. And isn't that what matters?

It's not a romantic outlook or what Hollywood would expect, but as long as it works for Coco and me, I'll keep it going.

When I look at my father, his gray eyes, so much like mine, brew a storm.

He's pissed.

Raw, hot anger flows through him.

I'm just a fuckup.

He couldn't be more disappointed in me. Would he understand if I explain to him why I have to do what I do?

An internal scoff reminds me who I am and who I'll never be.

If this were James, his older son, things would be different. My parents lost him before he was even born, but they worship him as if he was the best child of the four.

This shouldn't bother me, but even at my age, I'm still waiting for them to tell me I'm doing great and that they're proud of me. Dad only highlights my fuckups, and Mom stands by his side, agreeing with him.

"Is this why you called me?" I don't wait for his answer. Instead, I show him my phone. "Next time, text me."

"You don't understand the gravity of the issue."

I grunt. "Listen, I'll look into it."

"That's not enough." His voice booms throughout the kitchen.

"It'll have to be." I use my best passive-aggressive tone.

"Break up with her, or you're no longer part of The Organization," he threatens me.

I blink a couple of times and then laugh. It's a humorless laugh, full of sarcasm. "This is rich. You're going to take my toys away."

I quiver my chin like a five-year-old who's about to cry. One of the perks of being the grandchild of an award-winning actor is that I know a trick or two.

When I see that he's softened his facial features, I grin and say, "Oh wait, I don't fucking care."

With that, I leave the house. Once I'm in the car, I call Coco. Her voicemail picks up immediately. "You leaked another picture. We agreed you'd stop doing that… listen, I—" There's a chime on my phone, an incoming text. It's my future brother-in-law, Beacon. I cut the message short. "Just call me, okay?"

Beacon: *Can you give us a hand?*

Seth: *With?*

Beacon: *Teddy and Myles need some help with the wedding. Something about permits and working with the city. You know the right people to get them asap.*

Seth: *Are you getting married or playing a concert?*

Beacon: *It's part of the surprise I have for your sister. Can you please help?*

Grace is one of my favorite people in the entire world. Ever since I can remember, she's taken her role of big sister seriously, and I love her because of that and more. When it comes to her, I will do anything—even humoring her soon-to-be husband.

Seth: *Fine, I'll swing by Teddy's office to see what she needs.*

Beacon: *I owe you.*

He really does because visiting Theodora St. James is almost as painful as dealing with my father. So much for keeping away from the forbidden… I have to shut the rest of that thought down—I have a girlfriend.

But I can never stay away from Teddy. It's impossible, even though I know it's wrong.

Chapter Two

Teddy

HAVE you ever had the perfect morning?

For me, it's Mondays. I know, it sounds crazy, but Monday morning does it for me.

It's the day I get new requests, thank-you emails, and well, it's the beginning of a new week. It's like the first day of fall when the crisp air invites warm tea and a sweater. The beginning of spring when nature wakes up after a long winter.

Monday is the middle of summer, children playing in the park, ice cream trucks driving around the neighborhood, and swimming time.

I usually arrive at work before seven in the morning. Before heading to my office, I set the pastry I bought for Aaron, my assistant, on his desk. He's not a morning person and I believe that leaving him a little something might be a good pick-me-up. I don't dare bring him coffee because no one does it the way Aaron likes it.

When I enter my office, the sun is already shining through the east window. I set my latte and pastry on top of my desk along with my red Chanel backpack. I shed off my jacket and place it on the coatrack. Before I take out my tablet and laptop, I check on the landline's voicemails.

"T, this is Beacon. You should be getting help with those permits. Thank you for everything you're doing to make this wedding just perfect for my bride."

This is excellent news. I grab my latte and take a sip before sitting down. I go through my emails. There are a couple of requests for this week that I might be able to fit in without using the time I have allotted for the Bradley-Aldridge wedding. And no, I'm not the wedding planner, but I'm part of the event. My role is to bring Beacon Aldridge's plan to serenade his bride to fruition—to make it perfect.

This is my favorite part of what I do, making people happy. While growing up, I learned to please everyone and to fix problems. I like to bring solutions.

Mom says I have a unique gift for learning the traits of each individual and then giving them what they need. She wasn't surprised when I quit Dad's company and created my own— TPSJ Life Concierge. I cater to billionaires with unconventional requests. TPSJ doesn't stop there. I have all kinds of clients, and most importantly, I help charities—for free.

It's not an easy business to market. It grows by word of

mouth. Fortunately, having a wealthy and powerful family helps. Not that I use their resources, just their help spreading the word about what I do. They've recommended my services to friends, business associates, and whoever seems to require someone like me.

I'm a fixer-upper of sorts. I offer solutions, recreate dreams, and make people happy.

I'm good at what I do and thrive on it.

A few months ago, I helped my cousin, Lang, with his wedding. He had a great event planner, but he also needed a few things to make it extra special for his groom. After that, everyone in my family and our family friends have been asking for my help with their weddings.

Hence, I'm working with the Bradley-Aldridge event. They're friends of the family. As I'm about to text Beacon asking who'll be my contact, there's a knock on the door.

"It's open," I say, not looking away from the screen. "You're early. Why don't you get your tablet, and we can go through the to-do list? Before you say a word, no, we won't discuss the gossip column or Seth Bradley. I want to enjoy my Monday morning."

Aaron and I usually go through magazines and socialite articles to see if anyone could use our services. Today I want to avoid the task.

"Oh, was I on the agenda for the day?" The baritone voice resonating throughout my office paralyzes me for a moment.

Slowly, I look up, and instead of my assistant, I see *him*.

Tall, dark, and annoying Seth Bradley. The bane of my

existence. Damn it, why didn't I check who it was before I opened my big mouth.

His pale gray eyes narrow. "Hello, Theodora."

I stare at him for a few beats. Once I'm able to find my voice, I say, "Why are you in my office?"

He shrugs. "I heard you *need me*." The last two words make me shiver.

This man has the power to turn my world upside down every time he's around.

Do I need him? *We've gone through this many times. You. Don't. Need. Him. He's dirt under your shoe. Nothing.*

Then why is my heart beating so violently? Like it's about to push its way out of my chest and… I inhale a deep breath to try to settle.

Once I'm calm, I wiggle my fingers, tilting my head toward the door. "You heard wrong. Why don't you do us both a favor and leave?"

He grins, crossing his arms and leaning against the doorframe. He looks all sexy and fuckable. For just one moment I want to ask him to push me against the wall and… *stop, Teddy, Seth is not on today's menu.*

"But am I?" His arrogant voice turns me on instead of annoying me. "Because I got a text from Beacon stating the opposite. You need some permits."

I hold a groan. "Why you?"

"It's always me," he answers with an air of victory. "You think your cousin or your brothers are the ones who get that shit done?"

My jaw almost drops. The next time I see my brothers, I'm

going to kill them. They won't have time to write their last will. If only they knew about... I wouldn't tell them, but the last thing I need is to owe Seth Bradley a favor.

And what am I supposed to do now? It's too late to find someone else to help me. I stare at him as I figure out my next move. Seth and I have an ongoing game of chess. Loser ends up stripped and vulnerable. Winner breaks the other's heart.

I'm usually the loser.

Kick him out. Owing him a favor is like... But before I finish the sentence, I realize that, technically, this is a favor for someone else, not me.

My pride doesn't allow me to let him help though. "You can go, I'll find someone else."

The arrogant asshole uncrosses his arms and walks toward my desk. He takes a seat in the chair in front of me and gives me a challenging glare. "Really? Who is this mysterious person that'll come to your aid?"

"There are plenty of people."

He sighs. "Listen, as much as I'd love to turn around and let you deal with your issue, I can't ignore it. My sister's wedding has to be perfect."

Does this mean I win this one? I want to grin in victory, but I don't. He's right. This isn't about his annoying personality and the ways I hate him.

"Fine," I sigh, resigned. "Let me pull out the information."

Seth leans forward, grabs my cup, and takes a long sip of my latte.

"By all means, have some coffee."

He grins. "I thought you were offering."

"Why are you always so… so annoying?"

"Only for you, babe." He grins, blowing me a kiss.

I choose not to engage, and print the documents we need. While they're printing, I look up at him. He's staring at the newspapers on my desk. Okay, it's not only newspapers but also gossip magazines the receptionists bring every morning.

I like to stay informed. Unless said magazine has a picture of my childhood crush almost fucking his current girlfriend at a bar. Then, I want to burn them.

It's not as if I still like Seth that way, but there's something unsettling that makes me bitter when I see him with Coco LeBlanc.

"So, you follow me, huh?"

"No, I keep myself informed—it's my job," I remind him, but my mouth is loose and I blurt, "I heard you bought her a ring."

His facial features change. He's almost stoic. I call that agent mode—and I hate it so much.

"There's no ring," he says, picking up all the magazines and tossing them in the trash can that's under my desk.

"Well, when you're ready to buy her the ring, let me know. Tiffany's is too generic. When you propose to the love of your life, you should create something that's just perfect for her. I have several jewelers who can be discreet." I clamp my lips, annoyed at myself. Why am I offering to help him?

Fortunately, he doesn't answer, and my tongue just can't stop spitting words. "I also have people who can control the narrative. This can't be good for your family and…"

I press my lips together before reminding him there's an

entire company that might be in jeopardy if his face continues to pop up next to the infamous Coco LeBlanc.

He sighs. "I thought you said we weren't discussing me."

I don't know where I find the strength to say, "Of course not. I'm talking about the people affected by *your actions*."

He runs a hand through his short dark hair. "I can't control her."

I arch an eyebrow. "Who?"

"She's the one leaking the information."

"Coco?" My voice comes out a little too skeptical.

"It's not the paparazzi following you?"

He shakes his head. "I have people controlling that when we go out."

"That's… Why would she want to do that?"

He shrugs. "Most of the pictures the tabloids post are ones she takes with her phone or ones she asks her friends to take because *it's a great moment*."

I frown, and before I can stop myself, I'm searching for her online. Her last movie flopped, and so did her last EP. She used to be popular in her early twenties but was also a problematic star. I interned at a PR company for a year and learned a lot about her and her antics during that time. Also, I understand why she's doing it. It's a no-brainer.

"She's trying to revive her career by bringing in the Colt-Decker name."

He narrows his gaze. "Meaning?"

I place my hands on the desk and lean forward. This guy is super smart, but sometimes he doesn't understand social cues. "She's using your family name and doesn't care who goes down with her. Does she know about The Organization?"

He shakes his head.

"Maybe if you tell her—"

He stands up and walks back and forth a couple of times before he says, "She'll publish it and fuck everyone. I already have the death of one person on my shoulders. I don't need more."

I close my eyes briefly because he's talking about my brother, Archer. "He would hate to learn that you're still—"

"Don't start," he snaps. "I don't need another fucking lecture about how he would feel. He doesn't have any feelings, because he's dead."

Anyone would think he's angry, but he's not. He's hurt and broken. I know because every time I try to put him back together, he shatters even more and becomes more agitated and angrier. This time though, I don't react. I stay where I am, calming my need to do something.

Once I'm under control and I know I won't do anything stupid, I ask, "Why are you with her?"

Something flashes in his eyes before saying, "She's safe. Send me the information on what you need, I'll have it done by the end of the day."

"Seth—"

He turns around and moves his index finger between the two of us. "As you keep reminding me, let's keep our distance."

I look down at the trash can with plenty of images of Coco LeBlanc with him.

I should make a collage with all those pictures. A reminder

that he's with tall, athletic, beautiful Coco. Once America's sweetheart. I envy her, not because of her fame, beauty, or career. I'm jealous because she's enough.

She's worth Seth's heart.

He loves her so much that he doesn't care about his family's safety. I can only pray nothing happens to them.

Chapter Three

Seth

STANDING by the iron gate of a big property on Bainbridge Island, I pull out the invitation to my sister's wedding. This is a bad idea. Not the marriage to Beacon, I mean bringing Coco with me.

"This is ridiculous. I thought it was your sister's wedding," Coco complains when we go through the metal detector.

"Phone." One of the security guards opens a plastic bag already labeled with her name.

"I'm not giving you my phone," Coco protests. "I understood why I had to do it during the ceremony but now it's just abuse."

"Then you can't go inside," the guard responds.

"Do something, Seth," she screeches.

I grab her clutch and hand it to the guard. "Here you go. You'll have it before we leave."

"That can't be legal," Coco complains as the guard takes the phone out of the purse and gives it back.

"I told you not to bring your phone." In fact, I told her she wasn't invited, but it didn't seem to matter.

Why am I still with her?

I should've broken up with her last Wednesday when she came to my penthouse to "fix things."

While we discussed boundaries and hard limits—not sexual —she saw the invitation to my sister's wedding. After a long argument, it was down to having sex or taking her to the wedding. I chose the latter because I'm not attracted to her enough to fuck her.

To no one's surprise, my father is furious. Mom tried to be polite with Coco, but she wasn't convincing.

"I don't know why I bother. Your family hates me," Coco mumbles as we walk toward the open bar.

"They don't know you," I defend them poorly.

"You can at least introduce me to your grandparents." She reaches for her crystal clutch and then pouts. "When are they giving me back my phone? It's not like I'm going to live stream the event."

"When the wedding is over. I told you it was a media-free

event and phones wouldn't be allowed. I don't understand why you brought it."

"I can't believe they scanned me and searched my belongings like a criminal." Then she glances at Grace and Beacon. "Plus, you never told me your sister is marrying *the* Beacon... I'm missing the chance to get a picture with him. Do you understand what this would do for my career? What if I ask him to sing with me?"

She confirms what Teddy said on Monday. She's with me because of my family. I didn't care that we were using each other from the beginning. I help her control her image. She keeps me company. But there's more to her plans. She wants the Decker name.

My family, though, they're off-limits. As if I'm going to let her exploit them.

"Can you not behave like you're starstruck?" I ask, almost annoyed, while we head to the open bar. I need a drink before I snap and we end up in a fight that might upset my sister.

"I'm not. It's just a way to help me help them too. They should be honored to be around me."

I glance at her. "Clearly, they'll be fine without using you to push their career."

"You don't have to be sarcastic." Her snippy tone sounds almost screechy.

I'm tempted to text the security team, so they ensure that she doesn't get close to my family. This is exactly why I didn't invite her and now... well, now I don't know what to do with her. Theodora St. James would be giving me a lecture for being stupid and not thinking about what matters.

As if I invoked her, Teddy approaches us. Well, not us but the bar. She looks as beautiful as always. Unlike her brothers, she's not tall. Her brown curly hair is tied up into a bun, and the silver dress she wears accentuates her delicious curves. I can't stop staring at her and I smile when she finally spots me.

If there's a person who can brighten my life, it's Teddy. Not that I let her. I don't deserve her. And yet, I can't stop thinking of her—seeking her out.

"Who is she? And why are you staring at her as if she was a piece of meat?" Coco huffs. "She could use some liposuction and a good dietitian."

Teddy looks in our direction. Her head cocks slightly. She mutters something under her breath and plasters on a polite smile before saying, "Theodora St. James. I'm a family friend and also the owner of TPSJ Life Concierge." Within seconds, Teddy is pulling out a business card from her clutch. "Here, call when you're ready for an image makeover."

"I don't need one."

Teddy laughs. "Sure… maybe I'm wrong, and what you need is a new personality. I know a few coaches and therapists. We can fix you."

"Are you going to let her insult me?"

Teddy touches her collarbone. "Oh, did you think it was an insult? Forgive me. It's just my personality. I like to fix what's broken. I heard you need a new PR firm too."

I frown because why would she offer to replace my aunt's company? Coco stares at her clutch. "What about that drink?" Her voice is a slightly off tone, as if she wants to change the direction of the conversation and make friends with Teddy.

I could ask if she's still working with my aunt, but I don't. Why make this wedding more painful than it needs to be?

Teddy turns to the bartender and gives him a one-hundred-dollar bill. "Tequila, iced, and keep them coming. This is going to be a long night."

"Aw, you didn't bring a date. Well, I totally understand wanting to get drunk. Looking like that, no one would want to date you. Maybe you should be the one going through that makeover."

Teddy glares at her. "Hey, at least I don't have to hire a publicist to get me a pity date." Then glances at me. "Does she at least pay you well? I hope she fucks better than she fights."

She grabs her drink and walks away.

"What the fuck is wrong with you?" I bark at Coco.

"She insulted me. I wasn't going to—"

"Get the fuck out of here. We're over."

Coco's surprised look is priceless. I take out my phone and text security. "Someone will be here to take you back to the mainland."

"You can't be serious."

"Dead serious."

In less than a minute, a couple of female guards join us and escort Coco off of the premises. A moment later, Burke, my best friend, business partner, and Teddy's brother, is right by my side. I wish I could walk away, but I'm scanning the area, looking for his sister.

"I heard you finally took care of the trash," he mumbles.

"Don't," I warn him.

He arches a brow. "Are you heartbroken?"

"Nope." My brother Nathan joins us. "He's too pissed to talk. I always knew it'd be your Achilles' heel who'd get rid of her."

"What the fuck are you talking about?" Burke asks.

I don't stay to listen to either one of them since I find Teddy heading to the main house. She probably saw my cousin or the other owners and asked them for the code to have a moment alone. I grin as I spot her opening the back door. I'm right. I let her go inside before I follow. The perk of being part of the security team is that I have the codes for everything.

A moment later, I enter the building and head toward the second floor where the living area is. She's on one of the couches, hugging a pillow and holding her drink.

"Why are you here?"

"I'm sorry."

"You don't need to apologize for your girlfriend's behavior." She lifts her gaze, and her eyes lock with mine. "Why her? What's so special about her?"

"What are you talking about?"

Teddy huffs. "Never mind. I really don't care to understand you. I thought I did once, but as I got older I…" She trails her words and her gaze.

I walk toward her, grabbing the empty glass and the cushion. Then, I take her hands and pull her up. "Sorry."

"As I said—"

"I'm not apologizing for Coco, but for my behavior. I wish things were different."

"Please don't start giving me the speech." She pushes me

away and laughs. "This time, I don't even get to have sex first, just the apology and the long lecture on how you and I—"

She presses her lips together, hugging herself. "It's okay. I'll never be like her: cold, heartless, and mean. I'm happy with my body and with who I am. Now go back to your Barbie doll."

"She's been escorted off the premises," I say.

Teddy studies me. "Why now?"

"We might not be able to be together, but that doesn't mean you're not important to me. No one is allowed to hurt you."

She snorts. "You do it often."

"I'm sorry," I say, pulling her to me and kissing her hard, breaking my promise—again.

This has to end. I just can't let her go. It's not that easy.

Chapter Four

Teddy

MY ANGER MELTS away as he presses his lips against mine. They're firm yet tender. They envelop mine the same way his arms do my body. I should stop him.

I need to push him away from me.

Stop this insanity.

We've repeated this pattern since I was eighteen. We were in Vegas. A weekend of debauchery in the city where dreams come true. We kiss, make love, and fight because it's wrong.

Back then, I was too young. After that, it was the guilt of my brother's death. Or maybe it's because of Archer that he searches for me. I'll never understand what pulls Seth to me and then makes him regret me.

This has to be over.

I have to be strong.

But I can't tear myself away from him.

Seth Bradley has a claim. Some kind of ownership of my heart and soul. It could be just an obsession of mine—the lonely girl who can't seem to get anyone to love her, especially not this man.

Gently, he sucks my lower lip, and my internal struggle ceases. I slide my hands around the back of Seth's neck. My fingers push through his thick dark hair. I kiss him desperately, as if this is the last time we'll touch. The last time I'll allow myself to take what he'll never really give me.

Seth kisses me with the same intensity. We're two broken people trying to find a way to heal. No, we're two very stupid people looking for a magic tonic that'll erase the pain of our past. Sex between us is nothing but a toxic drug that'll make us forget but push us back to the hole of despair where we live.

I'll break again, but this time I'll find a better way to mend myself and care for my wounds. After I fall, I'll stand up and begin again. I won't lose myself—not this time.

This is the last time we're together, forever.

Seth caresses the back of my neck, trailing the tip of his fingers down my sensitive skin to my bare shoulders. His lips follow along, and his usual smell of wood and tobacco has a hint of women's perfume. Hers.

I remember why I'm upset, who he chose, and that I'm his second choice. That prompts me to push him away, to find the strength to reject him.

"No," I say, without knowing how to follow that word.

"Teddy." His breathing is hollow, his voice breaking. "Please."

"Please what? You want me to fuck you so you can forget that she left you. God knows how many STIs you carry after being with her."

"I never had sex with her."

A loud throaty laugh echoes through the room, and it takes me a second to realize it's coming from me. "You're priceless. I'll never believe those lines. Men don't abstain. Stop telling me it's only me—always."

"But it is."

"Lies. Men can't go without sex for that long."

The asshole dares to grin. "We don't go without sex for long —well, except this last time when I was trying to—"

"Is everything okay?" I hear a female voice. When I turn around, I spot Pria Decker, Mom, and Burke.

"Of course, everything is fine," I assure them because that's what I do. I tell people exactly what they want to hear.

"I heard there was an issue with Coco. Is there anything I can do to help?" Pria, who owns the PR firm that represented Coco, asks.

"It's taken care of," Seth says dismissively. "I hope you don't mind, but I ended things with her."

"As you should have done months ago. I told you it wasn't

necessary to stick around. I just needed you for a couple of dates."

Seth shrugs, and I'm confused by the conversation.

Burke is the one who steps closer and looks at me. "Are you okay?"

"Yes, I've been taking care of the mean girls on my own since elementary school."

"Then why are you here?"

"I needed a moment to compose myself," I answer with a partial truth because if I'm honest with myself, I chose to find a secluded place hoping he'd come to me.

Seeing him with her in the tabloids makes me want to puke but looking at them together in person made me physically sick. I wasn't kidding when I told the bartender to keep my glass full of tequila all night.

Burke looks at Seth. "Why are you here?"

"I thought she needed someone to be with her. She looked shaken."

"Next time, call one of us." Burke uses a threatening voice.

And, of course, it's at that exact moment when this becomes a circus because Fletcher, Myles, Kingston, and Zach arrive just in time to intimidate Seth. None of them care that he's some kind of martial arts blackbelt and can kill any of them with just a pen. I guess this is what happens when someone upsets their little sister. I'm lucky to have them, but sometimes it can be overwhelming.

"Everything is fine," I assure them.

"Is it? Because I heard that woman insulted you, and Seth

allowed it." Kingston, who is the oldest, walks to me and hugs me. "You okay, squirt?"

"I'm totally fine," I assure him.

He glares at Seth. "I'm disappointed in you."

"I'm sorry for what happened, Teddy. I really am." His voice sounds genuine. Unfortunately, I can't ask what he's apologizing for.

His girlfriend, kissing me, or not being able to love me.

Chapter Five

Seth

Isn't the wedding season over?

I complain as I read an email from Linda, my assistant, reminding me I have a meeting in ten minutes with the team assigned to Manelik Cantú's wedding. Manelik is one of Beacon and Grace's best friends and a security agent for The Organization.

Since he's famous and an agent, he needs tight security.

This is why I'll never get married. Well, that and the fact that the only woman I love is forbidden.

At the bottom of the email, Linda reminds me I have to wear a suit. No one pays me enough to do these crappy jobs. Three weeks ago, it was Beacon and Grace's event. In two weeks, it's Manelik's. What's next?

At this point, I wouldn't mind if Dad fires me or grounds me for the next couple of weeks. Maybe this is his way of making me pay for my insubordination—he's probably teaching me a lesson.

It's because of what Coco did to Grace. Coco didn't take any pictures, but she sold the news that Beacon married my sister. Her fifteen minutes of fame didn't last long. She pissed off the wrong people and is now blacklisted.

From what I heard, only four people have been blacklisted by the Colt-Decker family. She's one of them. There's the infamous Martin Levitz, Grandpa Chris's bandmate. The others are two names I don't recognize: Sky and Porter. I haven't had time to dig around those names. They must've done something as wrong as Coco to be on that list.

As I reply that I'll be there and start assigning positions, I get a call from Nate.

"Yeah?"

"Someone is digging up shit on your girl," he responds.

I straighten up and clear my throat. "Who are you talking about?"

If Coco is in trouble, I don't care. Unless she's dragging my name through social media. My lawyer is working on having her sign an ironclad NDA to ensure she won't do anything stupid. Maybe Dad was right, and she might get The Organization in trouble. I should've been more careful, but I wanted to try and…

What did I think I would accomplish by dating her?

It was just a couple of dates, but I saw it as an opportunity to move on from Teddy. Like that could ever happen. No one can take her place or erase her from my soul. No one.

"Why would I care if anyone is investigating Coco?"

"I meant Teddy."

"She's not my girl." I try to sound casual while I change screens and start typing her name into the search bar to see how much of her information is out there. Her company isn't one hundred percent public. Most of her clients come from word of mouth, even the charities she helps.

There isn't much about her online. Well, other than being part of the board of directors of her father's company, just like her brothers.

"If you're bored, go to Dad's office. He might have something for you."

He laughs. "We'll go with that. I'm bored, and she's not your girl. Listen, I don't care if you two are together. Nor that you can't seem to look at any other woman the way you look at her—ask Coco LeBlanc. However, I just wanted to give you a heads-up about the situation. But since you don't care, I'll go and mind my own business."

"Stop! Are you serious? Someone is digging into personal information on Theodora St. James?" I love my brother, but sometimes he has too much time on his hands, and he likes to pull pranks.

"I wouldn't bother calling you if it was a joke."

"How do you know about this?"

"I have a software that—"

"What did we say about hacking?" This kid is going to get us in trouble.

"I'm not hacking sh…" He mumbles something I can't decipher and says, "Never mind. I don't know why I bother."

Fine, I'll bite and humor him. "Who's doing the digging?"

"So, you want me to look into it?"

"Of course, I do."

"Well, you forgot the magic word."

I run both hands through my hair. He's laying this on too thick. "I'll pay you?"

"Nope, not that one."

I sigh. "Please."

"It's my pleasure." The arrogance in his voice makes my blood boil with anger.

I swear little brothers are so fucking insufferable. "You're annoying."

"Yet I'm the only person looking after you."

That makes me wonder one thing. "Why is Teddy on your radar?"

"Everyone in The Organization is always on my radar," he answers, taking a long pause. I hear the keyboard clicking on the other side of the phone. He's already working. "That includes their families and friends. It's a free service I give to our father in case anyone tries to fuck us up."

"Does he know?"

He scoffs. "You know what he'd do? Take away some stupid privileges even though I'm in my late twenties. He's ridiculous."

I agree, and though I want to side with Nathan because we're too old to be walking on eggshells when it comes to our father, I also don't want him to get in trouble with Dad. "Maybe you should try to follow his rules more often. Think about it. In the meantime, let me know who's digging and... I'll set some security for her."

"You're overreacting."

"What if it's some stalker who hired a sleazy PI?"

"Good point. I'll hack into her company's phone system and her personal number too. The second is just to change the location of her SIM card at all times so no one can track where she is at. I promise not to record or listen to any of her conversations. I'll keep you updated."

I should tell him not to invade her privacy, but he's doing the right thing. Maybe I should go and check on Teddy and ensure she's safe. I'll do it once I have her security detail assigned.

As if I don't have enough on my plate, my father calls me.

"Yeah?"

"I need you in the office."

"Though I'd like to be at your beck and call twenty-four seven, I have a company to run and assignments to fulfill."

"Delegate the wedding. I have a mission for the weekend with the A team."

"I'm not part of it."

"We're training new people to replace us. I need you there."

I think this is his way of saying he wants me to be part of his A team, but could he mean something else? Once, Grace mentioned he needed therapy to help him with his communication skills, and I'm starting to think she's onto something.

"Fine, I'll be there in an hour."

Chapter Six

Seth

BECOMING part of the A team is everything I wanted. I spend the week training with Dad, Uncle Harrison, and Uncle Hawk. Over the weekend, we go on a mission which is successful but leaves me drained. The next two days, I don't get a break. They take me back to one of the training facilities.

Wednesday afternoon, as I'm about to walk to my house, I spot Nate parking his car in my driveway.

My brother is a homebody. It takes a miracle to get him out

of the house, and the fact that he's standing only a few feet from me and looking like the world is about to end, worries me.

"What happened?"

He cocks an eyebrow. "You tell me. What happened in Vegas, *big brother*?"

I don't like the way he says the last two words. "Are you high, drunk, or... what is going on with you?"

"Vegas," he repeats. "Can you remember what you did there? Dig inside that magical brain of yours."

Listen, I don't have hyperthymesia, but I do have a photographic memory. They're completely different. The first is when someone can remember nearly every event of their lives with almost exact precision. The other is recalling images or scenes almost exactly from memory. I have that ability, and Dad trained me to use it from a young age.

"I can't remember my last assignment there."

He shakes his head and grins. "No, you went there during your twenty-first birthday."

"It was Archer's," I correct him. "That's almost... well, too long ago."

"What did you do?"

"Celebrate my friend's birthday?"

There was a lot more than that. I watched Archer's brothers behave like Neanderthals. I had to babysit their little sister and... well, I don't need to tell Nate what Teddy and I did during the weekend. If I have to blame anyone for my behavior, it's her stupid brothers who brought her along. Who does that? She was *just* eighteen.

Am I proud of what happened? I don't regret it, but... I'd

rather not bring up that weekend. It was the first of many times I hurt Teddy because I couldn't do more than just give her some moments.

I wish I could give her what she deserves, love. I just can't. It's for her own good.

"Why are you asking about it?"

He hands me a folder. "Congratulations, your tenth wedding anniversary was two months ago. I'm not sure if Mom will forgive you for not inviting her to celebrate your nuptials."

I glare at him before opening the folder. It's a marriage certificate from the state of Nevada. "This can't be real."

"Oh, but it is."

"You're just bluffing. Is this some kind of prank?"

"Do you think I didn't do my research? While you were playing favorite son with Dad, I spent time digging for information. It was filed two days after the wedding date. But that's not all. Turn the page over."

There's a second marriage certificate.

"Did you know Piper married Archer?" he asks.

I nod. "She told us when…" I clear my throat, trying to push away the heaviness of those days. It's almost impossible. I'll never be able to forget Arch, how he died because of me, or the fact that I broke so many people because of my carelessness.

I clear my throat. "Piper told me after he died. But Teddy and I… well, I don't understand. There has to be more than a certificate. We need proof."

"It was too long ago. It's almost impossible to find any footage. Are you sure you don't remember?"

I scratch my temple. "One hundred percent sure. How did you find this?"

"Remember I told you someone was digging for information about her?" He doesn't wait for me to acknowledge him and continues, "Well, that's what they found, along with a few ticket violations. Also, I figured out who dug up the information on your wife."

"She's not—" When did this happen? I try to think about everything we did during that weekend. Other than me taking her virginity.

If Archer were alive, he'd kill me, and Teddy's other brothers are going to make me pay. All five of them.

"How long will it take to give me a new identity?" I try to joke.

"You have a bigger problem." The seriousness in his voice tightens my chest.

I close the folder and ask, "What can be bigger than dealing with Teddy's anger and her brothers?"

"Coco LeBlanc."

"What?" I'm startled by his answer and confused. "She's out of our lives."

He shakes his head. "She's the one who went digging on Teddy."

"Why?"

"Probably because you spent most of Grace's wedding either staring at Teddy or antagonizing each other—like you always do when she's around. Or maybe... because the moment she insulted your wife, you finally kicked her to the curb." He taps his forehead a couple of times. "I'm guessing she wants revenge, and if she's not allowed to touch the Decker family, she's going to do it through Teddy."

"Fuck." That's all I can say.

"Do you still have a security detail with Teddy?" he asks.

I nod, but I'm at a loss, which is strange because I usually know what to do. "Where do I start?"

He shrugs. "I really don't know. Obviously, you need to annul this... or get a divorce. Okay, start with a lawyer. Then, figure out how you'll break the news to your bride."

I snap my fingers. "Piper."

"Might help you after she lectures you."

I glance at him as I pull out my phone. "Lectures me?"

He shrugs. "Pipe is always telling you that Coco is just—"

"Stop. I'm not with her anymore." I dial Piper's number. She doesn't answer, so I text her to call me as soon as possible.

> Piper: Is this important? I'm on the phone with Gabe.

> Seth: How's the good doctor doing?

> Piper: One of his patients died last night. He needs some cousin time, probably more therapy, and to rethink his career. We should plan on doing it this weekend.

> Seth: Today could work since I need to discuss something with you.

> Piper: Me? :confused face: emoji What did I do?

> Seth: I don't want to stir up memories, but I have a question for you.

My phone rings immediately. "Are you about to mention *him* who shall not be named but once a year and twice during holidays?" she asks without greeting me.

"Yep."

"Shoot, so I can fly to Seattle and cry on my cousins' shoulders. Then have Mom cook me chicken soup, and probably my dads will—"

"Stop using sarcasm as a way of evading your feelings."

"You sound like Mom, my therapist… and every other person who knows me."

"I'm going to ignore you and move on to my issue. Remember you told me you and Arch got married during the trip to Vegas?"

"Mm-hmm."

"Did you forget to mention something else?"

"Like?" The voice of innocence tells me she knows.

"I don't know… maybe my own wedding."

"I was hoping that wouldn't come up," she says, as if she forgot to mention that the flower pot broke or she ate the last cookie.

"Seriously, Piper? I'm married."

"It's not a big deal," she continues, not understanding the gravity of this issue.

"But it is. I'm married. I've been married for ten years."

"Listen, you two were drunk and decided to do it too. You

didn't file it, so why even tell you about it? Especially when she can't stand you, and you're an idiot."

"But we're married?"

"No. Not unless you filed it," she clarifies. "Which you didn't."

I look up at Nate. "Are you sure it was filed?"

"Yep, it was stamped almost at the same time as Archer and Piper's."

"Who is that?" Piper's curiosity has no boundaries.

Before she changes the subject, I say, "Can we focus on me for a moment? You can talk to Nate later. Who filed the documents for you?"

"Arch took care of it, like he always did." She laughs as if she remembers a joke or something about him.

I let her have her moment with her thoughts, which is too long. Once she calms down, she says, "I recall Arch mentioning something soon after the wedding."

"What was it?"

She clears her throat. "'I think I pulled the best prank in the world.' Do you think he…?"

"He wouldn't dare," I say, almost laughing at the poor imitation of Archer's voice.

"You two lived to prank one another… it might be possible that—"

"Fuck, I'm going to find him and kill him."

"Seriously, Seth?" She sounds hurt. "Just last week, while I played at the subway station, I thought I felt him, so don't joke about it."

We never found his body, and since he died, she has denied

that he's gone. She claims she can feel him. She can't come to terms with the fact that he's dead. If he were alive, I would bring him back to her, to his family.

"Sorry, I didn't mean—"

"So you're married? That makes you a cheater," she deflects the pain with an absurd comment, the way only she can do. I don't know if I admire her for her strength or should tell her to stop being in denial.

"Fuck off, Piper!"

"Who's going to break the news to Teddy?"

"Me, I… listen, why don't we get together this Friday? I'll find a jet to fly you from New York. Jude should be in town by then." I mention our other cousin—Gabe's twin. The four of us are almost the same age and were practically raised as siblings.

"You guys can help me figure out what to do while we give some support to the doc."

"That's doable. In the meantime, I'll call Teddy to soften her a little. She's not too happy with you after Grace's wedding."

"Teddy is never happy with me."

"Well, I would be pissed too if my husband didn't acknowledge me for ten years but is always asking for a booty call." She laughs and hangs up the phone.

Piper: *I might have the video of the wedding.*

Of course Archer recorded it, and I bet he has several copies around.

Seth: *Where is it?*

Piper: *There's an SD card on top of my nightstand.*

Chapter Seven

Seth

BEFORE I HEAD to Piper's house, I make a pit stop at my office. As I arrive at Range Communications & Consulting, I find Teddy going into the building.

I debate between going back home or just avoiding her. It's easy enough to avoid her, as her brothers' offices are on the other side of the fourth floor. However, as I turn around, I almost bump into Chloe, Burke's wife.

"Running away from your destiny?" she asks, wiggling her eyebrows.

"What?" I chuckle.

"It's pretty simple. Either you forgot something, or you're avoiding Teddy." She grins.

"Your husband is right. You have a wild imagination."

She rubs her swollen belly and smiles. "That I do, but I also know you have feelings for Teddy. You just don't want to admit that she's the love of your life, so you waste your time with... How's the starlet doing? Is she going to invite herself to my baby shower so she can ruin it?"

I cringe. "I'm never going to live down your birthday, am I?"

She shrugs. "Listen, we love you, and because we do, we want you to know that she's not the one for you."

"And you think Teddy is?"

"Probably, but she's always running away from you and you... well, when was the last time you had an adult conversation with her?"

"How can I when, as you said, 'she's always running away'?" I answer.

She shakes her head, linking her arm with mine. "Let's go and visit with Burke. We have a favor to ask the two of you."

I don't have time to humor her, but I also know she's just as stubborn as my sister.

"What kind of favor?" I ask, swiping my card to enter the door that takes us to the private area only Burke and I can access. "Does it require me to give you my kidney, or are you planning some extravagant surprise for Burke's birthday, and you need my help?"

"Good guesses, but my husband's birthday is not for another four months. Both my kidneys and all other organs are working properly, and I hope we don't need help."

"You're going to ask for something, but you don't need my help?"

"Mind-blowing, isn't it?"

"A little."

She pats my arm as we step into the private elevator. "You have some kind of superhero complex. Not everything is about fixing and solving other people's lives, Seth."

I don't know how to follow that up, but she does. "Maybe you should stop working as... What are you? An FBI agent, CIA, Interpol?"

"How did we go from one subject to the other?" I try to deflect the conversation. A few know about The Organization, and Chloe is not one of them. "Just the other day, I told Burke that you should be writing books and pitching them to Piper. She might publish it for you."

The doors of the elevator slide open on the fourth floor. Burke and Teddy are right in front of us. The moment Burke sees his wife, he moves toward her, capturing her in a tight hug and kissing her.

"Ugh, you two are sickly sweet," Teddy complains without acknowledging me. "Can we get this meeting over with? I have two more clients to visit, and one of them is on Bainbridge Island."

"Sickly sweet is not a real term. I'm surrounded by women

who like to make up shit," Burke complains and looks at his wife's belly. "Please tell me you won't be like *them*."

Teddy grins. "Oh my God, is that your way of telling us that you're having a girl?" she asks, clapping enthusiastically. "I hope Zach and Autumn's baby is also a girl. It'd be so adorable."

"We haven't announced it yet," Chloe whispers conspiratorially, rubbing her bump.

"Can we go to my office?" Burke asks with annoyance. "We have to talk."

I arch a brow. "Everything okay?"

He nods and turns around. We all follow him, and once I close the door to his office, he says, "We want you to be our daughter's guardians."

I glance at Chloe. "This is worse than a kidney."

"A kidney?" Burke frowns in confusion.

Chloe waves a hand. "It's not the same at all."

"You're just asking me to be in charge of your child for the rest of her life. How's that not worse than giving you an organ?"

"That's a little dramatic even for you." Teddy finally acknowledges me but doesn't look at me. "In my opinion, you only need one of us."

Burke claps. "Children, children, let's not start fighting again. We're hoping you'll never need to step up, but it's a just-in-case policy. If anything happens to us, our daughter will need a mom and a dad. From everyone we know, we think the two of you will be perfect."

Teddy looks at Chloe. "What about your sister, Anna?"

"I adore my sister, but she's always wanted to be an aunt, never a mother." She shrugs as if that explains everything.

"Don't get me wrong, I'm honored that you chose me, but you honestly think I'll be a good father? What about Zach, your twin brother? Or any of your brothers, for that matter?"

Burke gives me a knowing look. He doesn't need to remind me that Zach already has three children, and his wife is expecting number four. And honestly, I wouldn't leave a live fish or any other kind of pet to his other four brothers, let alone a child.

"You'll be great," he assures me. "Though we know you'll have the support of our families, we also realize the two of you are the best choices."

"Shouldn't people be married to become guardians?" Teddy asks, and I almost choke on my own saliva.

Burke frowns. "You okay there?"

Teddy sighs. "Another man allergic to commitment, how refreshing… Does your girlfriend know about your issue?"

It's on the tip of my tongue to tell her I'm married—to her. I bite my tongue hard and press my lips into a thin line while trying to come up with a response. I'm usually levelheaded, but when it comes to Teddy, I speak before I think.

"Oh, we hit something there, any problems with America's sweetheart?" Teddy continues.

My jaw tenses, and after a long deep breath, I finally say, "No, it reminded me of an issue I have to fix asap." I look at my watch. "As a matter of fact, we need to go."

Teddy waves at me. "I knew you wouldn't stay away from her for long."

"Oh, that is over. I said we as in *you and I.* I need you to come with me to fix an issue my brother found while I was out of town."

"Me? I'm here to help with the baby shower emergency." She points at Chloe.

"Oh, we brought you in under false pretenses. Anna has everything under control." Chloe grins. "You should go."

"I have things to do." Teddy checks her phone and kisses her brother on the cheek and does the same with Chloe before patting her belly.

"This is important, Theodora."

She glances at me with a warning. "Fine, just remember my rate is high."

"What happened to the friends-and-family discount?" I tease her.

"You're neither."

Burke groans. "Children, get along."

We step into the elevator. After the doors close, I step close to her and whisper, "We should follow your brother's advice and get along."

"Never. You and I are over."

I grin. "See, that might not be exactly true."

"What do you mean?"

Chapter Eight

Seth

THERE ARE three things I can't stop doing when Teddy is around.

Tease her.

Desire her.

And touch her.

As we head toward my car, I'm already holding her hand. I'm thankful she's not snatching it away because, for some weird reason, I need the connection between us. I need her touch.

"You should put a security detail on them," she mumbles.

"Who? Burke and Chloe?"

"Yeah. If someone looks after them every day for the rest of their lives, nothing will happen to them."

And just now it hits me; she's anxious and about to have a panic attack. Teddy can't handle losing another one of her brothers. No one in the family can. I release her hand and put my arm around her shoulders, side hugging her.

"They'll be fine. It's just a precaution," I assure her, kissing the top of her head.

"But maybe if you do something to prevent it..."

"Let's make a deal. We'll fix the issue I found today and then we'll try to figure out a way to keep Burke and Chloe alive forever, okay?"

"You're mocking me."

"Partially. I can't put them in a glass box forever." I open the door of my SUV and help her get inside.

"Where are we going?" she asks when I'm putting on my seat belt.

"Piper's house."

"She's in town? That's not possible. I just talked to her, and she was in New York."

I guess my favorite cousin came through for me. Maybe that's why she's coming with me willingly? "No, we're picking up something and then heading to my place."

Teddy crosses her arms. "Why?"

"It's a long story I'd rather discuss when we're in private."

"No."

"Excuse me?"

"You and I in a private place is always a bad idea. You know what happens... plus you have a girlfriend, remember?"

"Why do you keep saying that? We broke up at Grace's wedding."

She huffs.

"Theodora?"

"Tabloids, internet... pick your poison."

I groan. "What's out there?"

"A picture of you two strolling around New York, looking pretty happy."

"They're probably, old but still, Dad's going to kill me. I guess my lawyer hasn't gotten her to shut up yet."

"Don't you have people who can fix that?"

Before I can respond, my phone rings, the screen lights up with Byron Langdon's name.

"Aw, my cousin is calling." She presses the answer button. "Hey, Lang."

"Oh, you two are together. Did you decide to give the marriage a try, Bradley? I recommend you hide before I kill you."

"Not the time," I warn him.

"What is he talking about?"

"She doesn't know you're filing for divorce? I think that's pretty crappy, but with a public affair, I think she might be able to take everything you own—all those billions are hers now."

"Seth?" Teddy insists.

"We'll talk later." I end the call.

"What was he talking about?"

I tap the wheel while trying to figure out how to break the

news. Since there's no way to do it nicely, I say, "Honestly, I'm not one hundred percent sure yet. Nate found our marriage certificate."

"Our *what?*" She sounds dumbfounded.

"Marriage certificate," I repeat.

"This is a joke, right?"

I nod, getting off the highway and heading toward Medina, where Piper lives when she's in Seattle. "Probably a ten-year-old joke."

"What does that mean?"

I tell her what I know so far, finishing the story right as I arrive at Piper's house.

"She has a video of it?" Teddy sounds indignant, as if it's a sex tape. "This can't be legal."

"That's why I called my lawyers. Neither one of them has reached out to me. It's probably as simple as getting an annulment. We haven't lived together."

"I'm not a lawyer, but... I don't think that's how it works."

"We'll see," I say as I enter the code to Piper's house and disarm the alarm.

"Will Piper ever move on from Archer?" Teddy asks, holding a frame with a picture of the two of them. "It's been almost eight years."

"You never stop loving your first love," I answer with what Piper told me once while Gabe was mourning his high school sweetheart.

That was before Archer died. After that, I watched her try to let other people into her heart, but it seems impossible.

"That can't be true. Look at my parents. They've been in love so many times..." She trails her words.

"There's a difference between you never stop loving your first love, and you can't love anyone new."

"So you'll always love Coco, huh?"

"Why would you say that?" I ask, not stopping my pace. Piper's room is in the basement. Far away from the primary room that she used to share with Archer. One day, she'll be able to give away his clothes and maybe sell this house. Maybe.

"You've never been in a steady relationship until her. I assume..."

"Can we not discuss that, please?"

"They say communication is the key to a happy marriage," Teddy dares to say.

My phone buzzes. It's a text from Burke.

Burke: *Are you fucking kidding me?*

Seth: *What happened?*

Burke: *You married my sister?*

Fuck, I mouth.

"What happened?" Teddy looks at me with concern.

"Your family knows about us."

"Everything?"

I arch an eyebrow. "Would that be a problem?"

"It makes me look like a woman who can't stop her toxic trait."

I can't help but grin and cage her against the door. "Am I your toxic trait?"

"Keep your distance, Seth Bradley. You and I are finished. More so when you're with her."

"We broke up." I stare at the ceiling begging for... a little break.

"So you want rebound sex?"

"What tells you she wasn't the rebound sex?"

"I thought you said you never fucked her. Did you? And who do you need rebound sex from?"

I lean close to her. "From you, Theodora. Maybe I'm tired of this game and I'm trying to get over you. And no, I didn't sleep with her. It's always been you."

"You're the one playing with me—all the time. Each time we're together, you reject me."

"I—" My phone rings.

Fuck... "It's the lawyer."

"Aren't you going to answer? We need to get this over with."

And maybe I want to drag it out. "What if I don't want it to be over?"

"This is why I hate you, Seth Bradley."

I don't want her to tell me the ways she hates me. I enter Piper's room and grab the SD card. We head to the office and turn on the computer. When I put the SD card inside, I realize this is the first time I'm going to see a video of Archer since the last time we spoke.

Since the day he died.

Can I do this?

Chapter Nine

Teddy

ARCHER's gray eyes look at the screen with glee. He was always the happiest around Piper.

"I had no idea they got married. Did you?"

"I learned about it after he died. Piper told us it had been a last-minute decision. They had been engaged for three years. It made sense to take the next step."

"Without telling anyone?"

"You heard them. His favorite sister and one of his best friends were there."

But I don't remember. Why did they let me get drunk? "What about Piper's family?"

"My uncles and aunt wouldn't care as long as she's happy and he treats her right."

There's no more footage of the wedding, just some static. "We don't have answers."

Seth goes to the drive and clicks on another video. "Finally, you realize what I did. How long did it take you?" Archer laughs. "Weeks? Months?"

Archer pauses. "Listen, I'm sure you'll be able to find a lawyer to annul this marriage, but do me a favor and give it a try. This may sound corny and shit, but you and my sister have the connection. My brothers might kill me for letting this happen. I'll take their shit as long as you're good to her. I trust you."

I'm crying, not because of what Archer did, but because I haven't heard his voice in years. He was so young. I wonder if he'd look like our brothers or... "What happened to him?" I dare to ask what I've been afraid of for years.

Seth rises from his seat and paces back and forth, tapping his chest.

"Please, we deserve to know more than 'it was an undercover mission gone bad.'"

He looks at me and shakes his head. "It's classified."

"That's bullshit. You just don't want to tell us the truth."

"We were undercover." He pinches the bridge of his nose,

taking a few breaths. "They made us. We were escaping… One of us had to stay behind to trigger a bomb."

"Why him?"

He takes a deep breath. "He didn't give me an option. Archer chose for the two of us. While I was trying to think how to do it without putting either one of us on the line, he acted."

"How dare he do that?!"

Seth places his index finger on his top lip and stares at the image of Archer for a long time. After that, he says, "He had less intel about The Organization than me. If they captured him and he cracked, he couldn't give them much. If I did… it would have put thousands of people in danger."

"That's unfair."

"You think I don't know that? He didn't deserve to die. It should've been me. Every night I go through everything that happened and try to come up with a scenario where we could both leave. The nightmares continue every single night. He dies, and I'm here, undeserving of this life. It was supposed to be me, not him.

"He didn't trust me. We looked for him, his body… I still don't know what happened to him, how they might have tortured him, or if it was a painless death. Why do you think Piper believes he's alive?"

"She knows what happened?"

"Yeah, I had to tell her. It's complicated… and also the reason why she can't move on even though she's tried."

I clear my tears. "But what if he's alive?"

"It's been eight years. He would've been here long ago if he had survived."

"They might've kept him prisoner."

"When we went back looking for Archer, we killed everyone." He shrugs. "It's a rule. You don't leave any witnesses behind."

And maybe it's time for me to give up hope too. I don't know how I'll convince Piper to let my brother rest. He's been gone for so long. Too long.

I take out the card.

"What are you going to do with it?" he asks.

"I'll show it to my brothers. I think they might want to know about his last prank and move on too." I give him a half smile, while ordering a car through the app.

Seth's phone buzzes.

"Let it go to someone else," I say, knowing he receives the request. He and Burke created that application for our families, so we could give each other a car ride or run an errand.

"Teddy, we have things to do. You can't just leave."

I lift a finger as if saying, *stop it*. "This is what we're going to do. You're going to let me grieve my brother. Our lawyers will figure out how to get us out of this mess, and from this point forward, you'll stay away from me."

"Teddy…" He says my name with so many emotions, I don't understand what he's trying to say.

"This is for the best. We have to move on and find happiness." I don't know what that means, only that I can't continue waiting for him to love me.

Maybe he's been trying because his best friend asked him to do it before he died. I'm just some stupid promise to the death.

Chapter Ten

Teddy

MY BROTHERS ARE a bunch of idiots.

All of them—including Archer, may he rest in peace.

"You're right. This is perfect," Kingston says with a grin. "We finally got him. I knew there was a reason why Arch is my favorite."

"I thought I was your favorite," Fletcher, who's a big cuddly bear, complains.

"You are during football season," Kingston jokes. "Just like I am yours when you need groceries delivered. Now, tell me where we start."

"Excuse me, but I think you're missing the most important thing. I'm not going to be part of this stupid plan." I tap on the table where they have been piling information on what to do with this inconvenient marriage.

"Please," he says almost sweetly, which is some sort of a miracle coming from my oldest brother. "You can have anything you want."

"We never ask anything of you," Zach continues. "This is the best way to get back at him."

"Can you put yourself in my shoes for one moment? You want me to be married to a man who I can't tolerate just to continue a prank that makes no sense."

"It's for a few months," Zach says.

"Six tops." Kingston smiles at me as if that should be plenty to convince me to go along with this very stupid—just like my brothers—plan.

"No, and this is final," I say, looking at Fitz, my cousin by marriage, who happens to be a lawyer. "Could you please help me with the divorce or the annulment?"

"Are you seriously going to deny your brother's last wish?" Fletcher dares to ask.

This is the lowest of the low. He's using Archer's memory to entice me to go through with this crazy scheme. I look at the five of them and shake my head. Then, since Myles hasn't said a word, I ask, "Do you agree with them?"

He shrugs. "I'm the minority."

Well, he disagrees with them, but he's also not defending

me. I'm disappointed in all of them. They're usually amazing and supportive and… the best guys a girl could want as brothers. However, there are times like today when I wish I were an only child.

"I thought all of you were smart, but now… I think you're just a bunch of idiots."

"We could…" Lang trails his voice.

"Yeah?" Kingston tilts his head.

"Proceed with the divorce and fight to get some of his assets."

"You're not putting my company in the middle of this battle," Burke protests.

"Are you serious?" I snap. "Don't touch my company, but you can have my sister."

"That's not what I meant. You can make his life miserable for six months. Wouldn't you like to do that? It's not like you even care about him. I have to separate the two of you all the time. I'm handing you a way to make him suffer," he insists, as if it's logical.

And maybe if he knew how I felt about his friend, he wouldn't be bothering me. What would they think if they learned what had transpired between Seth and me?

"Stop it now." Myles's warning voice booms through the entire room. "As I said before, Archer did something very stupid. You don't play with people's lives like that, even if he did it because he was a corny bastard. Teddy won't be in the middle of your childish pranks. She's our little sister and we have to protect her."

"You're right." Kingston gives him a sharp nod. "I'm sorry

for trying to use you to get back at Seth. Fitz, can you work on this, please? Send me the invoice when you're done."

Fitz winks at me. "The first one is always free since you're family."

"Sorry, Teddy," Zach apologizes. "It was very insensitive of us to even suggest you stay married to him for our benefit."

Fletcher hugs me. "If I take you home and cook dinner, will you forgive me and make me your favorite brother?"

"I can do the same," Burke argues. "I'll feed you the best food in the country—even the world."

"You have a professional chef at home," Fletcher protests. "That'd be cheating. But if you take us both, it'll be a party."

"Okay, let's move this to Burke's place," Myles agrees. "It's better than having you littering my apartment."

"Our penthouse," Kingston corrects him.

Lang gives me a side hug and says, "Now that we know what to do, we can celebrate. We'll see you there. Teddy is riding with us."

Lang is the first to speak when we're in the car. "The only way to get an annulment is if you haven't consummated your marriage."

I don't understand what he's trying to say. "Excuse me?"

"There won't be an annulment, Teddy."

Great, my first divorce, and I'm not even thirty. "Can you find a way to make this an annulment? And how do you know we… consummated it?"

"If you two weren't fucking like rabbits every chance you get, I would agree."

As I look out the window, I say, "I don't know what you're talking about."

"Seth might think he's good at hiding shit, but you've been caught a time or two—after you fuck."

My cheeks burn. This is too embarrassing, yet I retort, "You're so crude."

"Someone has to give you a reality check, babe," Fitz says, turning his body so he can see me while Lang is driving.

"Well, it doesn't matter what you think Seth and I have done. I need this to be over."

"I might not agree with your brothers' idea, but I also know that you and Seth have something going on. Are you really set on just letting him go?" Lang's question hits me where it hurts the most, my heart.

"It's just sex." I don't finish the sentence with *for him*. It's just sex for him. It doesn't matter what I feel or want.

"Uh-huh."

"Either way, Lang is right." Fitz's blue eyes are so compassionate. I wish he was my brother or my father.

God, my dad is going to kill me. This is a disaster. But it won't be if I can convince Fitz to give the annulment a try.

"What is he right about?"

"I can't file for an annulment. It's been ten years, and you two have been intimate. However, the divorce won't take long. I'll start the paperwork while we have dinner so we can get Seth to sign it right away. After I file the petition of dissolution, it shouldn't take more than ninety days for it to be over."

But I don't want it to just be over.

Am I pathetic for wanting this to be real?

I wish the vows Seth said during our wedding were true. That he'd protect me and love me for the rest of my life.

Will I ever be able to move on and learn to love someone else?

Chapter Eleven

Teddy

ONCE UPON A TIME, I dreamt of being the wife of Seth Bradley. I was young and stupid.

Now that I'm an adult and my dream has come true, I have to figure out how to get rid of him. Divorce is simple, but what if I became a widow instead? Unsurprisingly, I can't sleep because I'm wondering what my parents are going to say about my wedding and my life.

Dad's already upset with me. I went from being Daddy's

little girl to the family's black sheep. Well, that can't be true. Fletcher, with his terrible career choice, is the worst of all of us. According to Dad, a football player is just a man waiting for a concussion and bankruptcy.

I wish my father could be less judgmental and more supportive. He's still hoping one of us will take over his company.

Since it's impossible to fall asleep, I google annulments and divorce in all the states. Maybe I can apply for an annulment somewhere else, like Vegas. However, it seems a lot easier to just file for divorce than prove to a judge that we're eligible for an annulment.

There's always another option, get rid of the evidence. Aka, my husband. I search for a million ways to poison a person without getting caught.

I go down the rabbit hole and read articles about women and men who attempted to kill their spouses. Most of them were unsuccessful and are now in jail. The idea of getting rid of Seth goes out the window.

When my alarm goes off, I get off the bed and follow my usual morning routine, though I add an extra shot of caffeine. It's going to be impossible to stay awake after eleven. When I arrive at the office, Aaron is waiting for me.

"Unusual," I say, handing over his morning pastry. "Did you sleep in the office?"

"Oh, sweetie, you haven't heard, have you?" He's pushing me away from the reception area.

"Now I understand why you never start the day before ten. You get weird," I say as we make our way to my office.

"Today is the exception, and just because I love you."

I turn around and give him an exasperated look. "What are you talking about?"

"Seth, Coco, and the other woman," he says, closing the door.

"So why do I care about this other woman?" It sounds salacious, and my curiosity piques. "Do we care?"

"You really haven't heard about it, have you?"

I wave dismissively. "Seth Bradley is not in my radar."

But as I approach my desk, I see a picture of me on the front of a tabloid. My pulse spikes. "What am I doing there?"

"Meet Seth Bradley's other woman," he says, arranging the magazines and newspapers with my picture and the headlines.

"No. That can't be me," I screech in panic.

"But it is, sweetie. Remember, if the internet says it, it must be true."

I'm at a loss for words and... what am I supposed to do?

My phone buzzes. I check my watch, and it's Seth. If he thinks I'm going to answer, he's crazy. We're done forever. I should tell Fitz to make the divorce painful for Seth. No, I should call Seth and make him fix this mess or...

Is he back with Coco?

"Do you know what this can do to our reputation?" I finally say something out loud.

"Nothing because you're going to call the best PR people in the country and ask them to handle this mess," Aaron says, holding my arms and shaking me slightly. "You need to take a deep breath and bring back the kick-ass, strong woman I know and we all love."

"Answer your fucking phone," Seth says, pushing the doors open.

"Oh look, my loving husband is here."

He cocks a brow. "Sarcasm doesn't sound well on you, Theodora."

"Neither does my name in the tabloids, and thanks to you, I'm as famous as Hester Prynne."

"She's not that famous," Aaron corrects me. "There are better classics than that one."

Seth nods. "He's right, but that's not the point. I called Aunt Pria. She'll take care of the PR, but we need to go."

His phone rings, and he huffs. "Yeah, Dad? Uh-huh, I'm at her office." He looks toward the floor-to-ceiling window and frowns. "What do you mean a helicopter? I just arrived ten minutes ago. It wasn't... I had to give instructions to Nate..." He nods a couple more times. "Fine, we'll do it your way."

Aaron walks toward the window and whistles. "Whew, that's a crowd."

"What's happening?" I ask, running next to him. There are vans and people right outside of the building. "Dad's going to find out about everything."

I hug myself, rubbing my arms up and down, trying to calm myself. It's impossible. My airways are clogged, and it's hard to breathe.

"Hey, I got this," Seth says, taking me into his arms. "Nothing is going to happen to you. I promise."

But he can't protect me from Dad's words, Mom's criticism, or the loss of my clients. My business is probably going to suffer, and what am I going to tell my employees? *Sorry, I can't pay you, but please don't leave me.*

"Trust me?" he asks.

I snort.

"I vow to protect you and make sure nothing happens to you or your business. I swear."

"Okay," I say, resigned. "Aaron, can you be in charge while I'm on leave for the next couple of days?"

He salutes me. "Of course, boss. We're here to support you. Everything will be fine. Maybe this will give a bump to the business."

Seth drags me through the building, taking Dad's private elevator. I'm not surprised to see Kingston heading toward his floor. He glares at Seth and then gives me a big hug. "Are you okay?"

"I'll be fine," I assure him, trying to build some strength.

This wouldn't affect any of my brothers. It shouldn't affect me, either.

"Where are you taking her?" he asks as the elevator opens on the floor that houses Earth Field Market's headquarters.

"Home for now, while we make a plan."

King nods. "I trust you."

"This time, I won't fail."

King pats his shoulder. "You didn't fail Archer. Stop punishing yourself."

"Dad?" I mumble.

"We'll take care of him, don't worry about it, okay?" King's voice is reassuring.

"Thank you."

He gives me a sad smile. "I'm sorry this is happening, squirt, but I'm sure everything will be fine."

After the doors of the elevator close, I ask Seth, "How bad is it?"

He taps his chest. "Just a few reporters who are trying to get the scoop. We're hoping our relationship doesn't come to light."

"We don't have a relationship," I remind him.

"I meant the marriage."

"Oh…" I growl.

"It's going to be okay," he assures me.

But not even he knows that.

Chapter Twelve

Teddy

SETH USUALLY PILOTS when we fly, but this time someone from his father's agency takes us to what looks like the middle of nowhere in the woods. I don't recognize the area. We could be in another country, maybe Canada?

From the helipad, we walk at least a mile to a big house. It's bigger than my childhood home.

"I don't recall living here," I say with a smart-ass tone. I'm being a little obtuse, but didn't he say he was taking me home?

"Your house is surrounded by reporters too," he answers as he taps a code on his phone and the house's main door opens.

This is a blend of rococo, English manor, and decadence. Seth's family is one of the wealthiest. I don't know who this belongs to, but they're loaded and... well, they don't like to have furniture.

As I study the two-story foyer and columns, corbels, ornate molding, and luxurious finishes of the structure, I wonder if we're invading someone's house or crashing some house for sale. "Where are we?"

"My place," he answers, making his way inside.

"This is a mansion. You own a freaking mansion, and it's... empty?"

He nods, almost proud of himself. "It's one of the most secure places I found in the area. The lot is big enough that I can have a small hangar and a landing strip." He shrugs. "It's practical."

Practical? I don't know how to follow that statement. In all my life, I've never heard anyone calling their house practical. It's like he's talking about a car with good gas mileage and a powerful engine. He doesn't care that the evergreens around it make the place magical or...

"Wait, so when you invite people—"

He lifts a finger. "No one is allowed into this sanctuary."

Then what's the point of owning it? "Why? And don't you live in a penthouse in Seattle?"

"Yes, that's where I sleep most of the time. This is my refuge."

"You're telling me not even Piper, Gabe, or Jude come to this house?"

He waves a hand. "They're different."

"Of course, they are."

He shrugs. "They are. Not many understand, but even though we're cousins, our parents raised us almost as if we were quadruplets."

"*All* of you Deckers were raised like siblings," I correct him.

"Yeah, but none of the others are almost the same age. Only the four of us."

"Will you do that with your children?"

He looks at me for a long time and then says, "I think my situation is too different to even contemplate something like that."

"Meaning?"

He shakes his head. "It's not important."

Why is he always so cagey? I don't ask him about his oddities. Instead, I bring up the most important question. "Why are we here?"

"I asked Fitz and Lang to join us since they had to speak to the two of us." He looks at his watch and grins. "They should be here soon. I wanted us to meet with them in a safe place. Until we control the situation, I want you here."

"I can be at home, where I'm comfortable." I eye what I think is the living room. The place is gorgeous but looks more like a museum or a mausoleum than a sanctuary. The windows are almost as big as the walls. If it was up to me, I would sell this place and build a house that's cozy and warm.

"How long do I have to stay here?"

"Probably just for a couple of days."

Where am I supposed to sleep? Does he own chairs or... "So, if I want to sit down?"

He points toward a big, carved wooden door. "The library is there. Make yourself comfortable while I get something to drink. You want a latte?"

I nod, entering the library and being taken aback by what is maybe the most gorgeous place I've seen in my entire life. It's a two-story library. There's a piano on one side, couches, and a small bar area in the corner. This is better than Beast's library, and it's real.

Browsing the books, I find several first editions of Isaac Asimov's books. It doesn't surprise me that the geek in him has this kind of literature in his office. As I walk along, I find more sci-fi books, including *Star Wars* hardcovers. One of them is signed by George Lucas.

"Here," he says, handing me a mug.

"That was fast."

He shrugs. "Did you have breakfast?"

"No. I left it in my office." I point toward the bookshelves. "Are those just sci-fi books?"

"Piper wouldn't let that fly. She's the one who's been filling the shelves." He points at the upstairs area. "There are thrillers on that side. Horror next to it. Romance is right beside the piano, next to biographies."

He has an entire library. I begin to scan the titles.

"How long have you had this place?" I ask after taking a copy of *Foundation* and sitting on the sleeper lounge chair close to the fireplace.

"Three, maybe four years." He shrugs.

"Keep your clothes on!" I hear Lang's voice before he and his husband enter the library.

"Hi." I wave at them.

They wave back, and then Lang says, "Have I ever mentioned this house is too fucking creepy?"

"As many times as I've told you you're not welcomed." Seth shrugs.

Lang ignores him and glances at me. "You can still ask for this property as part of the divorce settlement."

"I just need my freedom," I say, then ask, "Does Dad know?"

He sighs and his shoulders slump. "As much as I tried to avoid it, he did hear about your nuptials. He called me earlier asking if we would be taking care of the issue and to keep the press away."

I laugh, and Lang joins me. We love my father, but we also hate his male toxicity.

"Is he blaming me for this?"

"Probably. I didn't let him say more than the usual crap before I stopped him and let him know we would handle it."

"What are you handling?" Seth stands next to me.

"Your divorce, of course."

Seth looks at me, then at him. "Wait, you're already working on that?"

"Of course," I say, almost offended. "I want this over now. Somehow, people think I'm the other woman. What's next?"

He rubs the back of his neck several times before saying, "Well, Aunt Pria is using our marriage. The official statement will be that the wedding Coco attended wasn't Beacon's, but ours."

"That's a lie," I state the obvious.

"Yeah, but everyone will forget about us once they see we have nothing to do with Coco," he argues.

"I hate to agree, but he has a point," Lang agrees. "So you're saying we can't start the paperwork until things die down?"

Seth nods.

"While we wait, why don't you sign the paperwork?" Fitz finally speaks up. "We'll have everything ready, and it'll be over after ninety days."

Seth frowns, then glances at me. "Is that what you want?"

"Yes."

"Then I'll do it."

He doesn't sound convinced, but I don't ask him why he doesn't want to do it. Why read too much into the situation when it's useless?

Chapter Thirteen

Seth

So MUCH FOR no one being allowed in my house.

By noon, Teddy's brothers, part of my family, and even Bert, the family dog, are at my place. Mom is in the kitchen preparing food along with Grandpa Gabe. I'm able to avoid them by staying in my office and working.

Nate and I have been wiping Teddy's prints while figuring out a way to fuck the PI who gave the information to Coco. My brother already disabled her social media accounts and hacked her electronics. I understand all the laws we broke, but she fucked with Teddy.

Piper arrives right before lunch is ready. She hands me Helsey, her Havanese, and begins the hug fest.

"Jude will arrive in a few hours," she says, hugging Teddy. "Are you okay?"

"Totally fine. It's just another Friday in the life of Theodora St. James."

Piper chuckles. "That's the spirit. If you want to write a tell-all, I'll publish it."

"Teddy's Memoir, a tell-all?" I joke and relax, knowing Teddy is relaxing.

"There's my little ladybug," Grandpa Gabe says when he spots Piper. Then he looks at me. "You need furniture. Maybe we can order a few pieces so you have somewhere to eat?"

"Where's Grandpa Chris?" Piper walks to him and hugs him. "You look strange without him."

"He stayed with your uncle Mason. You know how he likes to control the media."

"Let me guess, he's in charge of the team that'll perform a PR miracle." Piper might sound repetitive, but I know what she's doing. She's distracting our grandfather from the fact that I don't own much furniture. He'll be on my case because just like Dad, he hated that I was with Coco.

Grandpa Gabe knows what it is to use and be used for PR purposes. When Aunt Pria asked me to do this one thing for her, he didn't like it. Thankfully, he hasn't said, I told you so. It'll happen soon, I just hope it's not until this mess is over.

Would they understand why the house is bare in some places?

This isn't exactly a home. It's more like... the Batcave. Bruce Wayne doesn't care if there's a dining table. Also, he doesn't have his family and friends barging in. Well, he doesn't have a family, but that's not the point.

When I'm here, I don't need to sit down and eat. I can just drink my coffee standing up or by my desk. Same if I prepare any food. On the days when Piper and the guys come over, we eat in the library. Eating pizza or sandwiches doesn't require a formal table or utensils.

"The food is ready. Where do you want to eat?" Mom asks.

I shrug.

She smiles and shakes her head. It amuses her that I don't have furniture. I wonder how she found this house and why she's here. So far, I haven't had time to talk to her. Not that I want to hear a lecture of any kind.

"We could try to eat buffet-style?" she offers, heading back to the kitchen.

"I'll help you serve." I follow.

"How are you doing?" she asks when the door closes behind me.

My eyes narrow. "That's a strange question."

"According to Teddy, you were in your office almost all morning." She cups my cheek. "You look upset. I just want to know how I can help either of you."

I lift my palms and shrug, as if to say, *I'm-at-a-loss.* "There's a lot outside my control."

She nods, as if understanding. I'm almost sighing in relief

thinking she's going to let it go, but I'm not that lucky. "You want to talk about your elopement?"

"Not particularly." With anyone else, I could get away with that answer, but this is Mom. She's not just going to let it go. If I don't say something fast, she's going to rehash the wedding and probably analyze the entire situation. "I watched it—on video. It's me, but I wasn't sober enough to remember. It's pathetic and stupid."

She nods as if it makes sense that I'm upset, but I doubt she understands the magnitude of the problem. I exchanged vows with Teddy. I promised to love her and protect her for the rest of her life. I plan on doing it. As a matter of fact, I've done it for a long time. However, when I said it, I didn't do it consciously.

I'm not saying that I dreamt of my wedding with her. I adore her, and even though it's impossible to stay away from Teddy, I still can't promise her anything. Each time I pledge to keep my distance, I fail miserably.

It's not lust that pulls me to her. It's the need to be with the only person who completes me—the woman who makes me feel alive.

Did it bother me to sign the divorce papers? Of course it did, because even when I don't believe in marriage, I thought that if I ever exchanged vows with Teddy, it'd be forever.

"You've always loved her," Mom says.

"What?"

"Teddy. You've been in love with her for a long time," she says. "I don't understand why you stay away from her, but I know your heart, and it belongs to her."

I shake my head, about to deny her allegations, but she gives me her don't-feed-me-bullshit look and I just say, "But we can't happen."

"Love is always possible." Mom says it with such compassion.

"It wouldn't be fair to put her at risk. I don't want her to end up like you."

"Like me?" Her indignant tone makes me straighten my back.

Did I say something wrong? This seems like the perfect time to bring up the obvious. "It breaks your heart each time Dad goes on a mission."

She smiles. "It doesn't break my heart. I worry about him the same way he worries about me. I'd miss him the same if he was some IT consultant traveling from one city to another or if he were just driving to the office."

"You'd be happier if he wasn't—"

"No. I think you're looking too much into it. Do I worry when he's on a mission? Of course, I do, but I believe in his abilities. The Organization makes your father happy. He believes in making a better world and knowing he's fulfilling his destiny makes me happy.

"I wouldn't change any of that. Maybe you need to rethink your priorities and your dreams. If The Organization isn't for you, then you have to quit."

I blink a couple of times. "But that's my legacy. Your husband expects me to step into his shoes."

She shakes her head.

"No, I don't," I hear my father's voice. When I turn around, he's almost next to me. "If this isn't what you want to do with your life, you need to let me know now."

I snort. "Of course, you don't expect anything from me. I'm not him, your prodigal son, the one who would've done everything according to you."

My father frowns. "What are you talking about?"

"Nothing." I toss my hands up in the air, giving up. I glance at Mom. "You guys can eat in the library. There's plenty of places to sit down in there."

I walk toward my office. Seconds later, Dad is right there.

"Are you here to lecture me?"

He shakes his head. "Why would I?"

"Because I fucked up again."

"Did you?"

"Just give me today's speech so you can move on."

He sits in the chair across from me. "There's no lecture. The woman you were dating seems to have trouble letting things go and likes to stir trouble to gain attention. I didn't see it until Grace's wedding, and I apologize for being so harsh on you."

I flatten my hands on the desk and lean forward. "What exactly are you doing here?"

It feels like some kind of trap or... my father never apologizes. Never.

"You left the kitchen upset. I've been putting this conversation off for years, but maybe it's time to talk about your role in The Organization."

I wave a hand. "Just let me know when you need me, and I'll be there."

"See, that's what I want to discuss. If your heart's not in what we're doing, then you need to quit."

"If I were him, you'd be finding a way to convince me that—"

"Who is this person you're referring to?"

"James."

Dad studies me, and once it hits him, he says, "You think that if he were around, he would've taken over the company."

"He's your favorite. You have him on a pedestal."

He rubs his forehead with both thumbs. "We have no idea what would've happened if he hadn't died. Losing him was painful. I won't deny it. We love him, but neither your mom nor I wonder what would've happened if he had been born."

Dad taps his index and middle finger against his lip for a while.

"Maybe of the four of us, he would've looked the most like you—" I pause. "Been more like you."

He shakes his head. "That would be impossible. He wasn't mine, but I loved him because he was part of your mom."

I'm startled by the confession. What does that mean? I do recall Mom had a boyfriend who abused her... was it him? Anger rises like bile. I want to know more and avenge her, but it's not the best time to figure out her past, is it?

"You should put that thought to rest," Dad continues. "And concentrate on what you want for your future. Do I want to leave my part of the company to you and Nate? I think you two would be great leading it into the future, but only if you're invested.

"If you see this just as some family chore that has to be

done because if you don't do it, no one will, then I need you out. Saving lives, wanting to make a better world, and helping others in this way has to come from your heart. Not from a sense of obligation. I do it because I'm passionate about it. If you're not invested, you're more likely to make a mistake."

"I've made several. Maybe you should fire me."

"Archer wasn't a mistake. It was a painful decision."

"He made it for me." My voice comes out too loud, too defensive. If I could go back, I wouldn't allow him to do it.

"Because he knew you wouldn't let him do it."

"Beacon almost died because of me," I remind him.

"Again, not your fault."

"I…"

"You need to take a break and rethink your future. The company is yours, but only if it's something you want to pursue. Do you understand me?"

"Why do I feel like you're dismissing me from being your son?"

"Because I probably made you believe that the only way I'd be proud of you is if you became my replacement." He scrubs his face with both hands. "And if that's the case, I failed you and I'm sorry. I never meant to force The Organization on you."

I'm speechless. "Will this ever get better? Our relationship?"

He smiles. "I was in my thirties when your grandfather and I were finally able to see eye to eye."

Dad rises from his seat, taps the desk once, and says, "Think about it. I love you no matter what you do. I'm proud of the man you've become. I'm sorry if I'm harsh on you, but believe me, I'm only half as harsh as my parents were with me."

Will the generational trauma we carry stop at some point?

I see him leave and wonder what I'll do with my life. Do I want to continue with The Organization? Is that for me?

Chapter Fourteen

Teddy

THE VISIT from my family and Seth's family distracts me from the tabloids. Mom doesn't say it out loud, but she's disappointed in me. Though, she tells me she'll handle Dad so he doesn't bother me for what I did.

The implication that I committed some kind of sin she'll have to fix made my stomach twist. Either she's going to find a way to fight with him, which will drag all six of us children into their toxic relationship, or... she's going to fuck his brains out.

Why can't I have normal parents?

If it had been only the two of us, I would've told her that technically I didn't do anything. It was my brother Archer. I think.

The memories of that trip are foggy. Vegas is so long ago. Okay, I do recall having sex with Seth—four times. But we both agreed what happened in Vegas stayed there. He had to go back to Boston. I was heading to Chicago where I was a freshman at Northwestern.

Everyone knows that long-distance relationships don't work. More so when he couldn't break the bro-code. That was the first of several times he used my brothers as an excuse not to be with me. And I stupidly took him back each and every time he walked back into my life.

But not again, I promise myself as I sit on the sleeper in the library to drink tea and eat some of the cookies Mrs. Bradley left for us.

My mom isn't bad, but sometimes I wish she could be a little more loving and understanding like Seth's mom. No, I think I like Piper's mom even better. It's so hard to choose among the Decker mothers.

"Are you okay?" Piper asks.

We're the last two people in the mansion. Seth flew back to Seattle to drop off a few members of his family and change helicopters. He promised to swing by Aaron's place to pick up my luggage. Aaron, who is not only the best assistant in the world but also a great friend, went to my house to get some clothes for me.

When I glance at Piper, she's looking at me expectantly,

even anxiously. "How can I help you?"

"I don't understand why I can't go back home," I answer, deflecting her question.

Who knows if I'll ever be okay?

"Seth wants to make sure the situation has died down before you step out in public." She gives me a sad smile. "I'm sorry this is happening to you. I feel somehow responsible."

I take a sip of the tea she prepared me earlier, and after a long moment, I ask, "About the wedding?"

"Yeah, I should've stopped it. But there's something about you and Seth that—" She shrugs and takes a deep inhale. "Arch and I used to say that you two would be the perfect couple."

I shake my head. "That doesn't sound like my brother. They're all protective, and when I brought guys home, they always pushed them away."

She smiles. "Seth wasn't just any guy. He was his best friend. If there was a guy he trusted with his little sister, it was him."

"How do you know?"

"As I mentioned, we used to talk about it."

"How? The last thing I'd discuss with my boyfriend is my sibling's love life."

She gives me a lopsided grin. "Arch and I were like an old married couple. Well, not exactly. There was nothing boring about our relationship. We did talk about our families and... well, you need to remember that, above everything, we were best friends. If something concerned us, we discussed it."

Arch and Pipe were my couple goals.

My brother worshiped Piper, and just as he treated her like a queen, she adored him just as much. And though what they had was perfect and unique, maybe she does need to start healing and moving on.

It's been eight years.

Eight years.

I dare to ask, "Will you ever allow yourself to fall for someone else?"

Piper looks hesitant, and when she finally speaks, she deflects the conversation. "Why are we discussing *him* again? It's not his birthday, our anniversary, or a holiday. You know the rules."

I roll my eyes as if saying, *you-are-ridiculous*. "I went to your house and it's like he hasn't left," I explain.

She waves a hand. "Just because I have pictures of him throughout our home, doesn't mean I won't give a chance to the right guy." She presses her lips together, hiding either a smile or her sadness. "Have you seen the dating pool? It's pathetic."

"What do you mean?"

"It's not easy to be single in the city—or any part of the world. It's a jungle out there."

And I hate to admit it, but she's right. Every time we wonder why she's not dating, we assume she hasn't moved on. But have we ever thought about the dating crisis? Dating is like going to a Starbucks and choosing from ten billion combinations. Even if you're lucky enough to find the one combo that might work for you, you may not be that person's choice.

Men my age are more interested in dating women like my mother. They have more money and experience. Most of all, older women don't want a commitment. They just want to have fun.

"We should try speed dating," I suggest.

Piper laughs. "Sure, because that's going to bring a non-desperate, well-adjusted man into our lives."

"At this point in my life, I'm just looking for *a man*," I joke.

"What are you two talking about?" Seth enters the library empty-handed.

My cheeks heat up, and I distract him by asking, "Umm, did you bring my things?"

He nods. "They're upstairs in the main room."

"Thank you so much."

Piper rises from her seat and shakes the cookie crumbs off her pants. "It's time for me to go home. When can I bail her out of this joint? I could use some shopping therapy."

Seth crosses his arms. "You hate shopping."

"Not for books. I want to check a couple of independent bookstores close to Silver Moon. They have amazing coffee and decadent pastries. She can't be held in the tower for the rest of her life. Even Rapunzel was allowed to leave."

No, she wasn't, but judging by her smirk, I guess she's trying to wear him down.

"I don't see why I can't leave." I try to sound calm, but my voice becomes slightly forceful. "Listen, I can take care of myself."

"Sunday," he says. "Hopefully, everything will die down by Sunday."

Piper grins. "I knew there was a marshmallow inside that hard heart of yours." She looks at me. "Be ready Sunday morning. I'll pick you up. We can go to brunch with my cousins and then book shopping."

"We could try Saturday," I suggest.

"No." Seth's warning voice makes Piper jump.

"You're an ogre. I'm going back to the city, but you know how to reach me."

After Piper leaves, I head to what Seth calls the main room. It's an entire apartment separate from the rest of the rooms. It has a study, a lounging area, a huge closet, and a bathroom the size of my condo.

The seven-head shower can be adjusted with a touchpad, and the towels are heated. I don't know where I'm at, but I don't know if I want to go back home. Once I'm dressed in a pair of lounging pants and a tank top, I go downstairs to look for Seth and find him by the stove.

"You cook?"

"You don't?" he responds, turning the knob and searching for plates in the left cupboard.

"Not often," I say, instead of admitting that I'm crappy in the kitchen.

Mom always had a cook. She never took the time to teach us how to… well, do so many things at home. During college, I ordered food when there wasn't anything good in the school cafeteria.

Once I moved back to Seattle, I had more choices, like visiting Mom or any of my brothers. My favorite place to eat is

Burke's. Chloe cooks extra and she's always happy to feed me when I visit.

"So you haven't learned yet."

"What are you preparing?" I change the conversation. My cooking skills are none of his business.

"Nothing fancy. Grilled chicken with quinoa Greek salad," he says as if it's something simple that anyone can cook.

"So, how long do I have to stay here?"

"As I said, by Sunday, you can leave."

"How bad are things?"

"Does it matter?"

"It's my life."

"Coco made a few videos playing the victim. We hacked the accounts to erase them and then close them. But as always, there's that one person who downloads the evidence before it disappears." He scratches his brow. "The official statement on the Decker website is I'm married, and my relationship with Coco ended months ago."

He makes it sound so simple, and I want to believe him, but... "She won't stop there."

Seth puts down the wooden spoon he's been using and turns to look at me. His gray eyes are brewing a storm. The kind of storm that ends up creating a consuming fire and havoc on my body. I take a step back, then a second one. With every backward step I take, he takes one toward me. When I bump against the wall, my breath hitches.

He moves some strands of hair from my face and leans forward, bending so his face is close to mine. So close I can feel his lips.

"Please trust me. I'm sorry you ended up tangled in this mess, but we'll figure it out."

And before he slants his mouth on mine, I scurry out of the kitchen.

We can't go back to being enemies with benefits, or... what were we?

It doesn't matter. I won't do it ever again.

I can be strong. Can't I?

Chapter Fifteen

Teddy

WHEN SETH CALLED me to dinner, I should've told him I wasn't hungry. Instead, as I approach the kitchen island, I feel like his prey.

Seth watches me.

His silver eyes almost sparkle like diamonds. Hard and cold —calculating. There's a rawness to him. His jaw is set, lips immobile. I'm waiting for his wicked grin to show, so the tension in the room diminishes, but nothing. His navy-blue cashmere sweater stretches over his broad shoulders. It's easy to make out every muscle beneath it. I know them almost by memory.

Every ridge, every tattoo, and even the scars he has on his torso. Probably on most of his body. I know too much about his body, even his breathing. That's weird for two people who only have casual sex because it's convenient or... I don't even know why we always end up fucking.

"Theodora." His voice is sharp, just like his eyes.

I gulp.

His tactile gaze tightens my skin.

I have to remember how to breathe and not ask him to fuck me.

My mouth is dry, and I suddenly have the urge to run. He's going to trap me. Even if I run far and fast, he'll find me, and I'll let him take me because when it comes to Seth Bradley, I'm weak.

Too weak.

"Sit down, and let's get started." He watches me as I take a seat on one of the barstools at the island.

There's a placemat, and the plate is already served, restaurant-style. It's almost perfect, but I'm not surprised. Seth does everything with precision. As if he's afraid to fail someone.

"This looks delicious, thank you for cooking, and I guess saving me from the paparazzi."

He takes a seat next to me and sighs. "I'm sorry for dragging you into this drama."

"You didn't know you were dating an attention whore."

He snorts. "I didn't even take the time to study her, or I would've known."

This time I'm the one who snorts because... "That's ridiculous. It sounds like you're saying that you should've profiled her before inviting her for a cup of coffee."

"That's exactly what I meant."

"Can you run that by me again? How do you know how to profile people?"

"I have a degree in criminology."

I can't help but look at him. "I thought you studied robotics or something like that at MIT."

He grins. "Among other degrees."

"You always find a way to make me feel dumb," I say, piercing a piece of tomato with my fork and taking the first bite of my food.

"When you have two parents who are overachievers, two siblings who are geniuses, and cousins who are just as talented, you try to at least keep afloat."

After chewing, I say, "That's ridiculous. You're just as smart and talented as your family. A lot of them look up to you, including Nathan. It's all about perception."

"You're wrong. Grace is a music prodigy, and Nate was able to talk to computers before he came out of the womb."

I can't help but laugh. Grace is super talented, and so are a few of his other cousins. Let's not mention that Nate talking to computers is a little far-fetched. "You have a knack for making everyone look better than you. Did you know that about yourself? Or maybe it's a way to fish for compliments."

He shakes his head and lets out an exasperated breath. Then, he reaches for a bottle of wine. "Would you like some?"

"No, thank you."

"It's your favorite."

I glare at him.

"What did I do?" The innocence in his voice is quite comical. "I'm just trying to make you forget that you're isolated until further notice."

Isolated with him of all people.

This close proximity is either going to make me combust, or I'll fall into his arms like I usually do.

No. This time is going to be different, I promise myself. I won't fall for his enigmatic personality and those commanding eyes. He has no power over me, and my heart is out of commission. I sent it on a one-way trip to Maui so it wouldn't mess up my head.

"So, you were saying about your criminology degree?" I pause, rethinking the conversation. I don't think I want to know about The Organization.

I learned the basics when Archer joined at sixteen. He and Seth had been the youngest recruits. Mr. Bradley needed them to go undercover at a school for a week. They had been training with him for years. My cousin Lang was already part of the company, and Dad trusted Arch would be safe.

And he was until he died.

I definitely have to change subjects, or I'll end up crying.

"A word of advice, if you ever have children, maybe let them have a life and not force them to study as a hobby." Yes, degrees and the schooling of his nonexistent children are safer subjects.

"We had a happy childhood." His devilish grin appears.

"Are you remembering those times you terrorized the neighborhood?"

His grin widens even more. "May I remind you that my only neighbors are also family?"

At least he didn't deny he was a troublemaker. "Exactly. Didn't you almost set your grandparents' house on fire?"

"It wasn't like that..." He releases a small laugh. "Well, it almost caught fire, but it wasn't our fault. Wade—"

"Who is Wade? And by our, I assume you mean the Decker terrors?" I think that's one of the names the Deckers gave Piper, Jude, Gabe, and Seth.

When they were four, Archer joined them, and he caused havoc right along with them. He learned so much from the terrors that sometimes he and Fletcher would destroy our house. I still remember the time he broke his arm because they were hanging from the chandelier.

"People have to stop calling us names. We were saints compared to our younger siblings. I guess they remember our antics more because we were the first ones. Wade was the family dog."

"What happened?"

"We decided to bathe him, but he ran away, and while trying to catch him, he went through the Christmas tree, and there was some electrical issue that created a spark and the tree burst into flames. Not our fault."

"Still your fault," I argue, and then I remember how fun it was to visit the Decker family.

The cousins might live in different houses, but they share an enormous backyard with a playground, a pond, and even skateboard ramps. During Christmas, they freeze the pond and recreate the North Pole. I got to see Santa every year. My house wasn't as fun, but we were always invited to the Deckers' for playdates.

"I miss spending the holidays at your house," I say.

"You should join us this year."

"No. This year it's Mom's turn to host Christmas. Next year Zach's and Burke's wives get to spend the holidays with their families."

"It's two weeks of celebrations at the Deckers'. I'm sure you can spare a few hours and skate on the pond."

I can't help but smile because when I was little, he and Archer were the ones who taught me how to skate. We continue eating in silence.

If we could keep this casual, friendly, and PG, I could endure the next couple of days with him. Right?

Chapter Sixteen

Seth

TALKING about my childhood should be safe, but it's not. Not when it brings memories of everything I've lost, my career, and my future. Then there's the conversation I had with my father. Am I happy with The Organization?

I like what it stands for, and I know we make a difference in many lives. Still, there are times when I disagree with Dad's decisions. The reason Nathan does whatever the fuck he likes is because he doesn't like our father's rules.

Just a few months ago, we had a case where we could've acted fast, but Dad and his partners wanted to drag things out to gather more evidence. That almost got Lang's husband killed. I understand they have procedures, but he should be more flexible with those rules.

Dad believes he knows it all and has the most experience. I wish he could be more receptive and listen to our suggestions.

"Are you okay?"

I don't know if I'm shaking my head because I'm trying to do the same with the thoughts, or just reacting to her question.

"You seem lost in thought."

"My father…" I pause, trying to remember exactly what he told me, but I just say, "He gave me a vacation from The Organization. He wants me to rethink my future."

"Are you unhappy with him or the company?"

I tell her why I've been on this track to try to become the perfect son. To have an advantage over James. If I can just push myself to be what my father wants, he can't catch up to me. Dad told me I could do great things for his company, but only if I'm invested in The Organization.

Am I?

"You probably don't want to hear about my existential crisis."

Teddy gives me a reassuring smile. "I don't see why not? You've done it for me several times. Like the day I transferred schools and then when I switched majors. There's also the time when you helped me move from Chicago to Silver Lake and then to Seattle. The time I quit Dad's company…"

She looks adorable when she sucks on her bottom lip, but

tonight I have to ignore all those quirks of hers and keep my hands to myself. Piper called me earlier to warn me. Either I pursue something solid with Teddy or let her go for good. Theodora St. James deserves more than a few intense moments.

Teddy deserves a man who dotes on her. Someone who understands her independence but also knows how to protect her. Someone who'll give her everything she needs. A man who will love her, and most of all, someone who isn't broken.

She doesn't need me, and The Organization might be better off without me. Even if Dad doesn't count my mistakes, I do. I know each one of them and how much it cost us. Just a few months ago, I dragged Coco into my life, and she's done her best to put many people I care about and me in danger. I knew better than to link my name to a starlet.

"You're being too hard on yourself," Teddy says, caressing my cheek. "I wish you could see yourself for who you are. A hero."

I scoff. "So much for being a hero. I got your brother killed."

"He'd be pretty disappointed in you."

"Why?"

"Because you're blaming yourself for a decision he made."

Teddy rises from her seat and kisses my cheek. "You. Are. A. Hero. Every time I need you, you're there for me. I think you have to start counting your wins and stop highlighting your losses."

I want to take her into my arms, hug her, and ask her to make me feel better. But I'm done being selfish. Until I can see my future and understand what I want to do with it, I have to abstain from taking the one thing I crave the most—her.

"Go upstairs." I don't mean for it to sound like an order, but my voice is commanding.

"Why? No. You're not the boss of me."

I take both of her hands and lock our gazes. "I'm more human than you want to admit. If you don't leave the kitchen, I'm going to bend you over and fuck you."

Her breath hitches, and her gray eyes turn a shade of green. I know what it means. She's wet and probably aching for me. This only makes me hungrier for her. I need her more than I need my next breath, but she deserves better.

"Teddy, we know this is a bad idea."

"It always is," she mumbles.

"Please, go to the bedroom or the library. This has to stop."

"I hate when you reject me."

"I hate myself even more," I assure her, leaving the kitchen and heading to the basement to train.

How do I stop wanting her when she's all I crave?

It's around midnight when I take a break. My body is exhausted, but I'm still restless. I check my phone and there are several missed calls from Piper. I dial her number right away.

"He's finally available," she says almost victoriously. "Who has Cinderella time?"

"Are you having fun at my expense?"

She laughs. "A little. We're having a big cousin slumber party. We miss you."

"Everyone is there?"

"Nope. Tucker couldn't make it since Sage is too pregnant to deal with the Deckers. I gave him a pass after he promised I'll be the godmother of their third baby."

I chuckle. Piper adores her older brother, and I'm sure she doesn't need to have a title to spoil Tucker's children.

"Why did you call me several times?"

"We wanted to know how you were doing. Also, I wanted to remind you to keep your paws away from Teddy. Plus, Dad said it's safe for her to come out of hiding. The press died down."

"I don't want her to be alone in her apartment."

"Then I'll take her with me."

That might be a good idea. She can be with Piper, and I'll head to one of the training facilities to think about my future. I'll leave a security detail with Teddy, just to be safe.

Chapter Seventeen

Teddy

I WAKE UP LATE, surprised I slept so much.

As usual, I reach for my phone and frown when I realize it's almost noon. I leap out of bed and decide to take a shower. Once I'm ready for the day, I make my way out of the room, wondering if Seth is around.

After he kicked me out of the kitchen last night, I never saw him again. This house is so big it probably has its own postal code, and it makes it impossible to find anyone. I should suggest handing a tracker to his guests. While I'm here, he could at least call me to let me know he's alive. *More like assure me that I'm not alone in his weird museum.*

My heart sinks when I enter the kitchen and he isn't there, but there is a note.

Text me when you're ready for breakfast. We're heading back to the city soon.

Seth

I feel slightly sad that I won't be near him anymore, but also relieved that I can go home. That's what he means, right? I'm allowed to go back to my apartment?

As requested, I send him a quick text. It doesn't take long for him to appear in the kitchen. He wears a black t-shirt and a pair of jeans. He looks delicious, but not as delicious as he does when he's wearing a suit or a tuxedo.

"I'm glad you rested," Seth breaks the sullen silence between us.

"Yes, thank you." I want to ask him where he was all night, but I decide not to do it. There are more important things to figure out, like, "When you say we can go back to the city, does that mean I can go home?"

He shakes his head as he goes through the kitchen collecting ingredients and utensils. "The commotion died down, but we don't think it's safe just yet. I want to give it a couple more days. Maybe you can go to work on Monday, and by Wednesday, you'll be back at home."

"Where should I stay?" My parents are not even an option. I could stay with either one of my brothers, but I imagine the best bet would be Fletcher since he lives in a gated community and has a bodyguard.

I had never heard of football players having security until my brother became the quarterback for the Seattle Orcas.

"You could stay at Piper's place," he says.

I like the idea. "Are you sure? I don't want to inconvenience her."

"She would be delighted to be there for you."

I know she would be. She's always been like a sister to me, and since Archer died, she's been trying to fill those gaps he left. I appreciate her, even though it's never going to be the same.

"Did she come back from New York because of my mess?"

Piper always jumps on a plane when she hears the St. James siblings are in trouble. She stays behind the scenes, but she's always watching. It happened when Zach's first wife died and also when he was trying to swoon Autumn, the love of his life.

She was there for Burke when he almost lost Chloe. She's part of our family. It worries me that when she finds someone, she'll forget about us, but if that happens, I'll understand.

"No. She's here for Gabe." He glances at me. "She needs an intervention."

"Whoa, how did we go from she came to look after your cousin to let's meddle in her life because she's doing something wrong?"

"What is she doing if she's not studying or working?"

I shrug because I've never asked Piper what she does with her day.

"She's helping others."

"And that's wrong because…" I trail my voice, waiting for him to finish with something logical.

"Piper doesn't have a life."

"She does."

"When was the last time she dated?"

I flip the question. "When was the last time *you* dated?" He looks at me a little baffled, though his lip curves into a slight smile. "What am I missing?"

"My dating life is what got you into trouble."

I snap my fingers. "You're the bane of my existence. How can I forget?"

He looks at me thoughtfully and then says, "If I ever get my shit together, would you give me a chance?"

His question confuses me, and I refuse to answer. I don't know if I'll ever give him a chance.

I'm free.

Not that I was in prison, but being somewhere in Washington State surrounded just by woods and almost no furniture wasn't great either.

I'm at Pipe's house, bags in hand, and looking at her looking like a wet dog.

"You're finally here!" she says excitedly.

"Where's Seth?"

I shrug. He had some guy I'd never seen before fly me back to Seattle. We landed at the headquarters of HIB securities, where another man waited to drive me to Piper's place.

It was very double-o-seven but without Seth's involvement.

"Please tell me he didn't switch me from one cage to another?" I ask Piper when I enter her house.

"Obviously not." She waves a hand. "I have an entire itinerary ready for us. As long as I make sure that we're not in busy venues." She rolls her eyes.

"Seth's rules."

"Yeah, he sent me a long text with all the rules I have to follow." Piper narrows her gaze and then says, "Do you know you have a bodyguard?"

"Yes, we met, but I don't want one," I almost screech.

She waves a hand. "It's just an added layer in case anyone tries to harass you. We won't notice him, I promise."

"Do you ever have security following you around?"

She shakes her head. "I'm well trained to defend myself. Plus, who would want to deal with me?"

"Your parents are famous."

Piper smiles as if that's not important. "No one knows about it. Plus, only two of them are famous. No one has any idea who Tristan Cooperson is, which is why I use that last name the most. No one cares about Piper C. Cooperson."

She and her brothers have one of the longest last names in the world. Bradley-Cooperson-Decker. Her parents are two men and a woman. Matt and Thea Decker are famous artists. Her other father, Tristan, is a billionaire entrepreneur who prefers not to be in the spotlight.

Piper is famous enough to need security, isn't she?

"How about when you play concerts? Piper Decker might need someone to protect her."

"It's just Piper, like Madonna but for classical music." She shrugs. "I don't have groupies. Actually, I sometimes play in the subway, and no one ever recognizes me."

"Why would you do that?"

She grins. "It has great acoustics, and I give the money to people who need it."

"You get money?"

Piper shrugs. "People toss money to me. What am I supposed to do? Ignore it? I collect it and then give it away."

"You're weird."

"And yet, you still love me." She smiles with amusement. "Why don't you take your things to one of the guest rooms? I'm going to dry my hair."

And I just realized her light brown hair is now teal and purple. She and her cousins have a thing for changing their hair color often. I've always wanted to be as bold as them, but Mom would have a conniption if I ever tried to change my hair or add extensions or… anything that's not natural is frowned upon by my mother.

Seth is wrong. Piper has a life. She lives it every day the best way she can. I wish I could be as independent as she is. Maybe I should be less concerned about making others happy and try to find myself.

Chapter Eighteen

Seth

"You okay?" Beacon asks.

"I've been better."

We're at my grandparents' house having lunch, as we do almost every Sunday. Not all the Deckers are here. Piper stayed with Teddy. I suggested they join us, but Pipe refused.

"We have plans for the day," she argued.

What part of "try not to be out as much" she didn't understand is beyond me. Piper claimed that yesterday no one disturbed them. This isn't LA, and once the paparazzi went back to California, the city became a safe area again.

However, she promised they were just going to go to a library downtown and later to Silver Lake—which is an hour south of Tacoma.

I shouldn't worry much since they have a bodyguard with them. But new stories and pictures surfaced about us. They're like weeds in the middle of summer. They keep popping up even when we killed them. I don't know when this will end and if we should just ignore it. Dad thinks we should look into it tomorrow.

"Come on, tell Beacon what's bothering you, little Seth."

Beacon has always been like a big brother or older cousin to me. We get along most of the time, and he's always looking out for me. It's easy to give him the SparkNotes of what happened within the past few days since he's aware of most of it.

"We'll skip the girl because you know my thoughts on that one."

I do. He's told me for the past couple of days that I should stop being stupid like he was and make a move on Teddy.

There's a huge difference between what happened between him and my sister and my situation. We'll never agree when it comes to my feelings for Teddy.

"What does The Organization mean to you?" The blow of his question leaves me startled for a second.

I respond with another question. "You said you were going to retire after you almost died. Why are you still working for Dad?"

His lips curve into a grin. "He calls us when it's extremely necessary. We built a great team, and even when Sanford can work with anyone else, he'd rather be with us. I don't have the right answer for you." He shrugs. "Sorry."

And he probably gave me the right answer. I have to quit The Organization. "My team is broken. I've never been able to rebuild it since…"

I don't know how to finish the sentence. It all started when Archer died and ended when Beacon was almost killed, and two of my men tried to kill him.

He tsks. "You know what your problem is?" Before I can snap at him, he continues, "You lost faith in yourself. If you took over The Organization, I'd follow you. We all believe in you."

"Dad—"

"See, that's the problem. If you keep looking for his approval before you even understand yourself, then you're fucked. Show him who you want to be, and he'll accept you."

"Is that what you did?"

He nods. "Pretty much. You have to show the alpha when you're ready to lead your own pack and leave him. Maybe that's not the best analogy, but you get my drift."

"What if he leaves The Organization to Grace or you?"

He pats my shoulder. "He's not ready to retire. When he does, he'll choose the best one of us. Probably you."

"There's Nathan."

He scoffs. "He's too volatile. I think he'll be good as a second-in-command but never the leader. You need to have more faith in yourself, trust your gut." He pats my stomach. "Trust that freaking gut and stop thinking WWMFBD?"

"What is WWMFBD?"

"What Would Mason Fucking Bradley Do?"

I laugh. "Does my father know how much you mock him?"

He shrugs. "I hope so. I never hide it from him."

At that moment, my phone beeps, and so does Beacon's. It's not just any sound. It's the emergency alarm for The Organization. I scan the room, and Dad is already heading toward the backyard and I assume toward his house. Grandpa Bradley follows him. Beac and I do the same.

When we arrive at his office, Dad turns on his computer and begins to work.

"What happened?"

He turns to look at me and grimaces. "The apartment building where Teddy lives is on fire."

My stomach drops. He doesn't have to say it. This isn't a coincidence.

"That's not all. There was a small explosion in your penthouse, but it was contained."

"Those are no coincidences," my grandfather, who trained Dad and is a retired Ranger, voices everyone's thoughts. "We need to act fast. First, send a team to guard the Deckers' estate. Then, we'll split into teams."

Beacon glances at me, and the look almost says, see-that's-the-man-in-charge-of-this-operation. He's right. Sometimes not even my father is leading the company, but my grandfather. But will I ever find my place in this company?

"Where is Teddy?" Grace asks, entering the office and walking into my arms. "I'm glad you're okay."

"Piper," I answer, pulling out my phone. "We need to check on both of them. Is her house okay?"

Dad clicks his mouse and nods. Then he scans the room. "Where is Nathan?"

"Still eating. He said to text him if you need his expertise," Grace responds, moving away from me and into her husband's arms.

"I called both, and neither one of them is answering." I turn to look at my sister. "Call Piper. Beac, try Teddy. I'm going to reach out to the bodyguard who's in charge of them."

He's not responding to his phone or my texts. When Dad says, "We have a man down downtown. There was an attack." I know it's the bodyguard in charge of Teddy. I just know it.

"Teddy?"

He shrugs. "Beacon, get your team ready. They're coming with us. Dad, move some assets to Teddy's and Seth's place. Grace, text Nathan. I need him to hack the CCTV around those three spots."

I don't wait for him to give me instructions. I jump in my car and go downtown to find Teddy while praying she's okay.

Chapter Nineteen

Seth

When I arrive at the scene, yellow tape surrounds an old bookstore. We're just a couple of blocks from Silver Moon, one of the nightclubs Piper's parents own. A couple of our men are scanning the area.

There are three bodies on the floor, covered by blankets. My heart stops until I realize they're too big to be Teddy or Pipe. I'm still holding my breath until I spot Teddy sitting in an ambulance where a paramedic attends to her.

When I approach, my heart sinks. Her clothes are bloody.

"Shouldn't she be on her way to the hospital?" The urgency in my voice makes the paramedic's head snap.

"It's just a small scratch," he says dismissively.

"The blood?"

Teddy sniffs, and I pull her into my arms. "It's okay, baby. I got you."

"Piper," she cries harder.

My chest tightens. "Where is she?"

"I don't know. Two men were trying to take us. One of them put a knife against Piper's throat." She gasps and cries harder.

"It's okay." I draw circles on her back. "You're safe. No one is going to hurt you."

Keeping my shit together is too fucking hard.

Where's Pipe? I can't push Teddy to tell me, but I'm praying my cousin is on her way to the hospital and her injuries aren't life-threatening.

"Piper tried…" Teddy sniffs. "She moved fast, kicked away the gun, and before I could run, there was a gunshot. She was on the floor. The blood." She looks at her arms and the tears continue cascading.

"It's going to be okay. You're safe," I assure her.

"This is her blood. It splattered when she was shot, and then the guy next to me fell too… I heard her say, 'Run, Teddy. Hide.' I ran to the bookstore."

"But where is Pipe?" I jolt at the growly voice. Grandpa Bradley is next to us.

"I don't know. She was on the floor," Teddy sniffs.

My grandfather shakes his head, almost crying. He loves us all, but he has a very special place for Piper.

Dad approaches, and Grandpa brings him up to speed. Dad taps his earpiece. "Nathan, hack into the CCTV and find Piper immediately. Have assets searching for her on foot and check Silver Moon. Maybe she's hiding there."

He points at the paramedic who's about to clean Teddy's arm. "No. I need a sample of that blood."

"Why?" I ask.

"I need to verify it's Piper's," Dad says, calling one of our technicians.

I'm impressed that the police are letting us do our own investigation. It usually takes days for them to allow us access to the scene or their files. With the fire, the explosion, and the kidnapping attempt, I guess they need our help to solve the case faster than they could on their own.

We're trying to recreate the scene while Nathan attempts to find some recordings of what really went down. We have three bodies. One of them is our asset, while the other two are unknown. We can't find Piper. The emergency vehicles only found the three bodies when they arrived.

I understand that the men who tried to kidnap Teddy and Piper killed our guy before they attacked the women. But who killed them? Was it Piper? Did she have a gun?

So, maybe Pipe shot those two men and ran, afraid the police would put her in jail before we arrived. No. It doesn't sound like her, but I can't find any other explanation.

"Who killed the other two?" I exhale in frustration. "We're missing something."

"A sniper," Sanford, one of Beacon's friends, responds, pointing at a tall building. "Both shots were perfect. If I hadn't been in bed, I would say it was me."

Sanford is one of our best snipers. He was taught by Uncle Harrison. He and Archer were his best students and later the best in his sniper team.

Dad narrows his gaze and sighs. "So we have a trained sniper in the city, and no one told us?"

"Nah," Sanford says. "If he's good, he left within seconds of killing these two, and he's probably already flying out of the city—or the country. Canada would be the first place I would go."

I stare at him dumbfounded. Not once have I heard that part of the plan. He has worked for me several times and I never discussed that with him.

He shrugs. "At least that's how Everhart taught me to handle things if something went wrong. Don't wait for anyone. Get the fuck out of there."

Sanford is definitely onto something. We're trained so well most of us just react by instinct. The first thing he does in any job is to get off the roof and immediately make his way out of the scene. If his team is in any kind of trouble, he can't intervene. Also, he should fly out of the country.

"So, where is Piper?" I ask again.

"If we figure out who those two work for, we might learn who was trying to kill them," Dad says. "My gut says this was a personal attack against The Organization."

He doesn't say what everyone is thinking. It was about me. I fucked up. I scrub my face down with one hand. "Who's our enemy?"

When the police officers are bagging the bodies, I glance at one of them and see it. "Stop!"

"You can't get close," one of the officers says. "We're doing enough by letting you be on the scene."

"Glove?" I ask, ignoring him.

Dad hands me a silicone glove and puts one on himself. When I move the neck of the man, I see it clearly. The skull tattoo with a Z and a cross next to it. Most of the members who belong to Los Zamudio Cruzes cartel have it on their neck. At least those who belong to the family by blood.

"Let me see the other man," I order before they move him, and I see the tattoo there too. I look at Dad at a loss. "But we…"

I can't finish the sentence in front of all these officers. They won't react well if I say, "But we killed all of them."

It happened while we were searching for Archer. We made sure no one was left behind. There wasn't a trace of them. They are…

"Piper," I whisper, knowing who has her.

They took her, and they might be hunting us. I can't breathe knowing they took her. What they'll do to her, and what they'll do to Teddy if they get a hold of her.

"We'll find her," Grandpa Bradley says, his voice almost breaking. "We have to find my Piper."

Dad's eyes darken. "Yes, but we might have bigger problems. Let's all go back to headquarters."

"Someone needs to start searching for Piper," Grandpa

says with a trembling voice I've never heard from him in my entire life. "We have twenty-four hours before we lose trace of her."

"Nathan is on that," Dad says reassuringly, squeezing his father's shoulder. "We'll have her home in no time."

But are we going to find her alive?

I hate that we're at headquarters piecing everything together instead of in the field. Didn't we just do that while we were at the scene?

My head is here, but my heart is with Teddy at the hospital. Anyone would think I chose work above her. I didn't.

We have to figure out our next steps to keep her safe. We'll probably have to send her off grid along with our families. We believe they found us because of the social media shit show Coco LeBlanc set in motion the past few days.

I hate proving my father right. This mess put a target on everyone's head, and we don't know where to start.

Worst of all, we can't find Piper.

"I don't know what happened after the first guy was shot." Nathan shows us the video on the big screen. We can see from different angles the first time he was shot. He fell on top of Piper.

We don't think she was killed, but she might've broken a bone during the fall. I won't be the one telling her parents we lost her—and it's my fault. Archer would kill me if he were alive. Or maybe none of this would've happened if I... But I can't return to that day or bring him back. We have to focus on saving my family and keeping Teddy safe.

"Someone tampered with the surveillance footage around the area," Nathan explains. "They replaced it with old footage of the same area. I don't know if they put Piper in a van, carried her off, or if she ran away and she's hiding."

He shrugs, but I can see the anger in his eyes, the frustration. "Whoever is behind this is two steps ahead of us and a genius."

"It's not the cartel," I say. "That's what Archer and I did for them. Unless they found someone better."

Nathan's jaw clenches. "I'll find him. There has to be a signature in the encryption ."

"You never leave a signature," I remind him. "What makes you think this person does?"

"They found her belongings in the bushes," Dad announces. "They took her. She didn't run away."

"Why her?" Grandpa asks, trying to be strong, but I can see he's about to lose his composure.

My airways are almost clogged, but I say, "Archer always had a picture of her with him. Maybe they saw her?"

The sudden silence is asphyxiating me. No one wants to say it, but we might never see her again. And if we don't want to lose anyone else, we have to hunt them down.

This is war.

Chapter Twenty

Seth

I T'S BEEN twenty-four hours since the incident.

We have teams searching for Piper, but there's no trace of her. The entire family is devastated. Though she's our priority, we also have other things to figure out, like keeping the rest of the Decker family safe.

We haven't slept much, but we came up with a plan.

"It's crazy," Dad says.

"Unorthodox," I correct him.

"The only way it can work is if you use Teddy," Nathan points out.

"No." My voice is almost a growl.

"You have to," he insists.

"What if something happens to her? I can do it myself, but dragging her with me is…" I don't finish the sentence. If I die, it's on me, but losing her… That's not an option.

"She needs to be part of this, or it won't work."

He's right. The cartel knows she's important to me. Isn't this why they took Piper? Because she mattered to Archer? And if they did their homework, they know she's my cousin. I feel sick to my stomach just thinking about what they're doing to her. We lost the twenty-four-hour window to trace her.

My guess is Piper's already somewhere in the Amazon being tortured, if not already dead, and they disposed of her body the same way they did with Archer's. I try not to dwell on it. Not now. I have to ensure that everyone else is safe, and once I dispose of every person who hurt her, then I'll grieve.

Still, taking Teddy is risky, and I don't think I'll survive if I lose her.

"We could use a decoy," I suggest.

Dad's look is unreadable. I'm waiting for him to suggest something and chime in, but instead, he crosses his arms and observes me.

"You have to trust yourself, the plan, and the team behind you for this to work." Beacon, who's been surprisingly quiet, finally speaks up.

Crossing my arms, I give him a challenging look, almost saying, stop-saying-the-same-fucking-thing. "I trust myself."

"If you did, you wouldn't mind bringing Teddy along," he argues.

It's so simple to say that. Anger surges through my veins. What if the one person who means the world to him... I stop, because Grace has been part of his team since she was sixteen. As far as I'm concerned, he's never had a problem taking my sister on a mission. Never.

But there's a huge difference between my sister and Teddy. That's the perfect excuse not to take her with me. "Theodora St. James is a civilian. She doesn't have any sort of training. She could be a liability."

Having feelings for her is a disadvantage. That's exactly why they're after her. The cartel knows she matters to me. If I bring her with me, we're doomed. Aren't we?

Beacon shrugs an arm. "She can run, hide, and follow instructions. You don't need her to handle a weapon. The question is"—he leans closer, narrowing his eyes—"can you separate your emotions from the mission? That's what might fuck the entire operation."

I glance at my father, hoping he has another solution.

"I'm not concerned about you carrying a civilian," Dad says. "It's the whole plan in itself. You want the cartel to believe that they're chasing you, while we're chasing them. The mouse always knows they're at a disadvantage. They know they're the prey."

"You're wrong. They're cocky enough to believe we're at their mercy. Also, they want Teddy and me. We leave, and they'll follow us."

He nods and adds, "They probably want the rest of us too."

There's no proof that they know about The Organization, but I understand why my father is already two steps ahead, wondering how he'll protect not only the family, but all his guys too.

I tap on the list. "The evacuations begin tomorrow morning, Dad—" Well, some. Mom is already tucked into a secure place along with my grandparents. My father wanted Grace to follow them, but she refused. She's one of the people searching for Piper.

Even the St. James family is evacuating. Piper's parents want to stay inland until they find her. Grandpa Bradley is in charge of convincing them that it's best for them to leave.

Dad lets out a long breath and glances at my grandfather, who nods. "Fine, we'll do it your way. I'll leave the A team in the city with several men while Beacon's team backs you up. What do you need from us?"

We spend the next few hours tracing what will be our escape route, the weapons I'll bring with me, the vehicle, and the safe houses we can stay in while on the road. However, I have to plan on using motels to drag them out in the open.

"Now, the hardest part." I scoff because we've been planning for so long, but we forgot one extremely important thing.

"What is it?" Dad looks at me, puzzled.

"Teddy hasn't agreed to be part of the plan."

We look at each other, knowing that if she's not in, this might not work, and we're running out of time.

"You're shitting me." Kingston's voice is so loud Burke's house shakes. "She's not doing it."

"Oh, but I am, big brother," Teddy argues.

"Don't you see what's happening?" he snaps at her.

I step in front of her. "Calm down and never speak to her like that. I understand we're all stressed—"

"Stressed? Try fucking scared. My family is in danger because of you." The vein on his neck throbs. "And you dared to come to us asking for her help?"

"It's the only way to end this."

"Didn't you end it when they killed my brother?"

"Stop." Burke pats Kingston on the back. "Archer joined The Organization aware of what could happen to him. It was his passion. He died doing something he believed in, and it's no one's fault."

King huffs. "Okay, I'll give him that. I never blame anyone for *his* death. But Teddy joining them—"

"Might be the only way to drag these people away from the city." I match his tone. "If we don't act fast, there'll be more casualties, including your family."

"Are you done with your testosterone match?" Teddy pushes me aside and stares at her brother. "I appreciate you, but I'm the one who decides if I stay or go."

I give a sharp nod. "The lady is right. We'll do whatever you want."

Secretly, I'm hoping she'll say no. I trust everyone on the team, but what if something goes wrong? I would never forgive myself if she dies.

"I'll go," she answers without hesitation.

"No." King's voice echoes throughout the house.

"Can you stop screaming?" Teddy pokes him in the chest. "We can talk like civilized people. Now, if you have a better idea to bring Piper back home and keep everyone safe, please enlighten us. If not, stop meddling."

"Who cares about Piper?" he scoffs.

"Archer did, and you do. You love her like a little sister. Just a couple of hours ago, you were trying to come up with a way to find her."

Kingston sighs. "But I don't want anything to happen to you."

Teddy glances at me. "I trust you'll keep me safe."

Someone might as well have stabbed me in the chest. Seriously, she trusts me? After what I did to her brother? And Beacon's words come back: I have to believe in myself for others to do the same.

If I want this to work, I have to stop thinking of everything that'll go wrong and start trusting myself.

"Teddy," King whispers her name. "We can't…"

He doesn't finish, but I know what he wants to say. We can't lose you.

"She'll be fine," I promise.

As King is about to say something, Burke chimes in, "We trust you."

"Let's go. We have to get you some equipment before we begin the trip."

Teddy hugs her family.

"Dad should contact you soon. Get ready to evacuate. You won't be taking anything with you, not even your vehicles."

Kingston scrubs his face. This is extremely difficult for him. He's always been the one deciding everything for their family in the absence of his father. I have no idea where Donovan St. James is, but I'm glad he's not around, or we would've had a big fight.

He still hasn't forgiven me for killing his son.

Donovan isn't the only one who hasn't forgotten about it. I don't think I'll ever forgive myself for what happened to him, or what Piper is going through because I fucked up eight years ago.

Chapter Twenty-One

Teddy

"Are you sure about this?" Burke asks me as he hugs me tight.

"Of course." I sound so casual that no one would believe I'm trembling and seconds away from having another panic attack.

I've been shaking since the moment that guy put a gun to my back and told me to be still or he'd kill me. His voice. I can't forget his words. They're playing in my head. The smart thing to do would be to run or hide with the rest of my family. Let the professionals figure out how to get us out of this… what is this?

Suddenly it's like I'm no longer in Washington. Instead, I'm somewhere in the Middle East because I've jumped into a *Jack Ryan* episode, but Seth is much hotter than John Krasinski. The difference between the show and my life is that real people are going to die. All my neighbors lost their belongings and almost died yesterday because of the fire this cartel set in the building.

Piper is in danger. Pipe, one of my best friends and my sister. I can't stomach the thought of losing her. Archer would want me to help Seth. We need to find her, and if I can do something to help with that, I will. That doesn't mean I'm not terrified about what could happen to me if anything goes wrong.

"I trust Seth," I say out loud, reminding myself that he knows what he's doing, and he would never let anything happen to me. "He's your best friend. You should trust him too."

"I do," Burke says, giving me one last hug.

When Kingston embraces me, he mumbles, "I don't like this."

"Have faith, okay? You need to be strong for the rest of them."

"The wait is going to kill me."

I pat his cheek. "You're an impatient man. Maybe this is some kind of teaching moment."

He huffs. "What am I supposed to learn?"

I shrug, kissing his cheek. "We'll see when everything is over."

"Take care of yourself, okay?"

I squeeze his arm. "You take care of Mom and make sure everyone is okay while you wait."

"Time to go," Seth announces, squeezing Burke's shoulder one last time.

I wave. "Tell everyone I'll be fine and that I love them."

My brothers nod. I'm sad that I don't get to say goodbye to anyone else, but also happy because I couldn't bear seeing their faces while leaving.

We don't speak until Seth pulls out of Burke's garage.

"Why did you park in his garage and not outside?"

"I didn't want anyone to know I came to this house or that I'm bringing you with me," he answers.

"They can see the car and trace it, can't they?"

He shakes his head. "No. The windows are completely tinted. The plates are stolen, and if they've been keeping track of me, they think I'm downtown, sleeping in my hotel room."

"That sounds pretty elaborate."

"Thank you for agreeing to do this with me. We tried to devise a plan that wouldn't involve you, but it was impossible."

"It's the least I can do."

"What does that mean?"

"Piper. If I hadn't pressured her to take me out of her house—or even leave your mausoleum, she…"

"They would've found another way to get to you and to her."

"I don't think they wanted her."

"Why would you say that?"

"One guy clearly said, 'What do we do with the colorful peacock?' The other guy answered, 'We rape her and kill her. We don't need her.'"

"Are you sure that's what they said?"

"Yes. They talked a lot."

"Why didn't I think about asking you what happened?"

"Probably because I was hysterical."

"Are you okay?"

"Not really, but I'm trying my best. You know what they say, fake it until you make it. If I pretend nothing happened to me, I might be able to stay calm."

"I'm so sorry about this. If I had been more careful…"

"Though I appreciate your apology, you have to stop it. You had no idea your crazy girlfriend would put you and everyone you care about in danger."

He nods.

"What are you not telling me?"

"It was bound to happen."

"What do you mean?"

"These people are the same ones who killed Archer. I thought we had eliminated everyone, but we didn't. They started a different cartel. Nathan found a lot of information about them."

"He googled them?" I joke.

He snorts. "Of course not. He has some underground forums for mercenaries."

"That sounds dangerous and highly illegal."

"It is, but he knows what he's doing."

"So the same guys who killed Archer might've taken and probably killed Piper?"

"I thought they wanted to torture her since they realized who she was. After what you told me… I don't know what to think."

He doesn't want to admit that they disposed of her. Once I think of those words, I start crying again. She's my big sister. One of the most important people in my life. She has to be okay. There has to be hope for Piper.

"How are we supposed to get past this?" I sob. "How are you not sad?"

"I can't afford to be anything right now, Teddy. I can't think of what happened to her or if I'll ever see her again, or if I might lose more people. My father, grandfather, and anyone involved with this operation is doing their best not to think about her right now. We will when we know everyone is safe."

Seth reaches for my hand and holds it until we approach the HIB headquarters building. "You can still say no, Teddy. This isn't your battle."

But it is. Those men killed my brother, and they might've killed Piper too. If it's up to me to stop them, I will do my best. "As I told you at Burke's house, I trust you."

When he parks, he closes his eyes briefly and then looks at me. "This might be hard for both of us. I know you like to challenge me, but you have to do everything I say. Can you do that?"

"I only argue when it's something you're wrong about."

"Not always," he claims. "There are times when you just want to make things difficult."

I grin. "It's fun to see you upset."

"Well, as much fun as it is to fuck with my head, can you not do it during this mission?"

"Only if I can do it once we're safe."

He laughs, and that sound makes me relax a little. He takes off my seat belt and drags me to his seat. "It's a deal."

"We have to keep our hands off each other." I try to sound firm, almost threatening, but it comes out all needy and wrong.

He shakes his head. "Believe me, we won't have time to do anything more than drive and try to stay alive while the team behind us takes care of the cartel."

"What if they don't take the bait?"

"They'll be there." He brushes my hair away from my face. "Though, I believe they don't know about The Organization or who I really am. They believe what Coco told them and what they can see. I'm just the CFO of Range Communications & Consulting. Some stupid geek who's rich and took money from them."

"And that's good?"

He grins and nods. "That's perfect. It means there are fewer people in danger."

I wiggle my way out of his seat before I kiss him or ask him to make me forget everything that's happened.

"Then let's begin this road trip and make sure there's not a single one of them left this time."

I sound so optimistic even though I'm willingly walking into what might be my end.

Chapter Twenty-Two

Teddy

"ARE you sure you want to do this?" My cousin, Lang, is asking as Grace is giving me armor, wigs, and other gadgets that might be helpful during this road trip.

"It's not like you have other options," I answer.

Grace freezes and smiles. "There's always a second option."

"I thought Seth said—"

"My brilliant brother didn't think about one detail." Grace touches her sternum slightly. "Me. I can pretend to be you."

"Before you start throwing out ideas, stop," Beacon says as he enters what looks like a storage unit or the big closet for The Organization.

"Don't go all alpha on me, Aldridge," Grace protests, walking toward her husband and hooking her arms behind his neck. "You know it would work."

"Not when I need you to be a part of my team. I can't spare anyone. If we want to replace Teddy, it would have to be another operative, and I don't trust anyone else to do a good job." Beacon's explanation makes sense, and in a way, I feel better knowing that my cousin and his friends will be the ones looking after us.

"Listen, it's not like I want to color coordinate, but is this all I can wear during this trip?"

Grace shakes her head. "No. I'm giving you what you need to wear during the car drive. When you're at the hotels, you can wear whatever you want."

My cheeks heat up in embarrassment. It's not like I want to be a pain in the ass, but maybe they don't remember that I don't own anything. Not even a toothbrush. Last night I used my finger and a drop of toothpaste.

"Aaron already did the shopping for you," Lang says, as if reading my mind. "It's just the basics for the trip. Once things are back to normal, we'll make sure to get you into a new apartment. It'll be like nothing was ever lost from your life."

"Thank you." It's hard not to tell them that I'm not concerned about the material things but all the memories I have from my family.

There were pictures of when I was a kid, back when

everyone got along, including my parents. We used to be a happy family, and I was the only one who had physical proof of it. Other than the picture in my office, I don't have any of Archer. All the presents he and Piper gave me are gone.

"What's going on with Piper?"

Grace leans her forehead on her husband's chest, closing her eyes. Pain etches in her facial expression. I want to apologize for losing her cousin. If I had trained just a little like Archer or all the Deckers, maybe we could've fought those men.

"We're still searching for her," Lang says reassuringly. "We'll bring her home."

I don't know if he's saying that to make me feel better or for Grace's sake. He sounds just as calm as Piper did while we were under attack. Not once did she panic. When she told me to run, she said she'd be fine, to trust her.

It's just now when everything hits me. The peace in her voice sounded as if she really had everything under control. Is that how people react when they're about to die? A way to reassure the other person that they'll be in a better place?

She knew that she couldn't get away, didn't she?

"You can't go into a mission when you're all emotional and shit," Lang interrupts my thoughts. "We understand this is difficult, but you have to lock all those feelings in a box until this is over."

"Listen to the cold asshole. He's an expert." Beacon laughs after saying that, and Grace does too.

My cousin is one of the most loving and loyal people I've known. I have no idea what they're talking about, but maybe he's different during missions. Can I turn off my emotions?

It'd probably be for the best, as I have to resist Seth. On second thought, this is a terrible idea. Close proximity with Seth Bradley is going to kill me. We already tried it in his mansion. Now we're going to be cramped in a car and living in hotels together.

How am I supposed to keep my body and my heart tamed? Who is going to survive when we fight? He's going to drive me crazy, and I won't be able to walk away.

This is a bad idea.

The worst.

"Everything okay?" Seth asks when he enters the room. "We need to get this going. The sooner we leave, the faster we can start evacuating people."

Lang looks at his watch. "I have some calls to make. There are a few changes I have to make before I go to Luna Harbor."

"Is your team going to be ready?" Seth looks at Beacon.

"We are in position. Just because one of us will join in a different state doesn't mean we're not ready," he snaps.

Seth raises his hands. "Whoa, aren't we a little sensitive?"

Grace rolls her eyes. "You two are impossible. Come on, Teddy. We have one more stop before I drop you off where you're supposed to meet Beacon."

"What does that mean?"

"No one knows you're here. They still believe you're in the hospital where the paramedics took you."

I frown. "But I was discharged."

She grins. "Yes, but one of our assets stayed in your place, making everyone believe that you're still there."

"You guys are good."

"We are, but you can still say no," Seth says. "This is your last chance before we begin the mission."

A billion emotions are piling up in my chest and my head, but if anything, I have to be strong for everyone else. Mostly my family. Maybe by doing this, we will find Piper. They haven't promised that, but what if we find the cartel's headquarters, and she's there, safe?

"You might need to remind me what matters and that my feelings should stay here in Seattle. I'll be scared at times, but I want to do this. As I told you earlier, I trust you."

He hugs me. "Nothing will happen to you. I'll see you in a couple of hours."

Chapter Twenty-Three

Seth

GRACE IS A CHAMELEON.

When she changes her appearance, she's unrecognizable. I watch her load the car she's taking to the hospital. Teddy gets in the back seat. She's also wearing a disguise. Once she changes places with the asset that's pretending to be her, I'll be going to pick her up. We're beginning our journey.

Of course, as I'm about to leave, Dad and his business partners are stalling.

"It's going to be okay," I reassure my father.

"The last time someone was hunting us, one of his children almost ended up a quadriplegic." Uncle Anderson, who's been working with Dad since The Organization started, points at Beacon. "You need to understand why he's being cautious."

"Knowing that the cartel hasn't made us is a relief," he says. "Still, we have to keep it that way. There are operatives here, but what if your backup needs backup?"

"We can always join them," Uncle Harrison says.

"I don't want three old men backseat driving us," Beacon protests.

Since they won't be on my case but watching after us, I say, "Sure, why don't you do that. I'm sure Beacon can use a few extra sets of eyes."

"If you don't die, I'll kill you." Beacon gives me a threatening glare.

Not many would understand, but this kind of banter relaxes me. It feels normal. There's tension, and everyone is nervous, but we're trying our best to focus on the mission. Since the clock is running and it's almost time for me to go, I glance at Dad. "Can I talk to Mom?"

He nods, pulling out his second phone. He's the only one who can reach most of the people who are off the grid. Especially Mom.

"Don't tell her I'll be part of the mission." He gives me a sheepish look.

This could be a perfect moment to give him a hard time.

It's so perfect that Beacon is the one who jumps to it. "You shouldn't lie to your wife, Papa. Keep those lines of communication open or your marriage might fail." His mocking tone makes my father groan.

"Please don't antagonize the boss." Harrison uses a warning voice, but I hear the underlying humor. He's a lot like Beacon in that aspect. Always giving Dad a hard time. "That's what I do during missions, and I won't allow you to take away my fun."

Beacon salutes him. "No, sir. But if you need backup, I'm here for you."

Fuckers, Dad mouths.

I stop paying attention to their nonsense and dial my mother. "Mason?" she answers immediately.

"It's me, Mom."

She exhales. "You're going, aren't you?"

"We have to do it."

There's a long silence before she says, "Stay safe, okay? I love you very much."

"Love you too. I'll see you when I'm back."

She makes a noncommittal sound before asking, "Have they found Piper?"

"Sorry, Mom."

She releases a small sob but recovers fast. "Come home soon, okay?"

"You got it. Love you."

I hand the phone over to my father. "We're all set. Don't forget to call her if you plan on joining us."

Dad's eyes are reserved. They don't give away anything. He might not confirm if he'll be on the road until I see him or when we're back in headquarters. And for once, I hope he decides to ride along.

He taps his chest, and after a couple of deep breaths and a sharp nod from both of his friends, he says, "Let's get ready. We're joining them."

Normally I would tell him he was only joining because he didn't trust me. This time, I don't. I need all the help I can get to keep Teddy alive and end the cartel once and for all.

As I arrive at the hospital, I spot two of my men guarding the entrance. There's a woman by the vending machine fighting with it. Once she notices me, she follows me to the elevator. We're the only ones who board it. That's when I notice it is Grace.

Knowing no one can hear us, I grin and say, "Your father is joining the mission."

She glares at me, as if to say, *you're-an-annoying-little-brother*. "Stop harassing me."

I shrug innocently. "But I'm not. It's the truth."

"Please tell me you're kidding."

"Nope." I cross my heart. "This is as serious as a heart attack. The three old men will be there to help. You should be thankful Uncle Tiago is on hiatus."

"What are they going to be doing?"

I shrug. "Ask your team leader, he's the one in charge of them." I can't help but smirk when she understands the meaning of it. She'll be working with our father.

The elevator doors slide open, and I walk away, knowing I

annoyed the hell out of my big sister. I don't like when Dad is hovering, but she loathes it.

"Ready to go home?" I ask when I enter the room.

Teddy is already changed into a pair of black cargo pants and a shirt. To anyone else, she's wearing regular clothes. I know she's wearing the armor. I hand over the jacket I brought for her. "It's slightly chilly outside."

The nurse who's helping us says, "Here are the discharge instructions. You should contact a counselor soon."

I grab Teddy's bag and the papers before we leave the room.

"Whoever was in my place looked a lot like me," she says. "No one noticed the difference."

I doubt anyone looks like her, but we have excellent makeup artists who can make miracles happen. Once we get in the car, she asks, "Where are we going?"

"Along I-5."

"To California?"

"We'll stop there if necessary, but if our calculations are correct, we might be going all the way to South America."

"Are you insane? That's a long trip."

"No. We're trying to drag them back to their turf." This might stop before we reach the Mexican border. There's a team heading to what we believe is their territory. They'll be scouting the area. Dad and the others will decide if they want to send more people and attack at the same time we take down those who might be following us.

"And you're going to fight them all?" She chuckles. "I think you're forgetting that I only know a bit of self-defense and carry a small can of pepper spray."

"We'll have plenty of backup, I promise."

"Can I ask you something?"

"Shoot."

"While I was in the hospital, I read that Coco LeBlanc is in jail. She's being charged with the arson at my apartment and the attack against me. Probably the death of your cousin. How?"

He grins. "We had evidence that she hired a PI to dig for information about you. Nathan gave enough evidence to the police to make it look like she's one of the suspects."

"That's a little vindictive."

"Yes, but we're also doing it so the cartel thinks we have no idea they're behind those crimes. We're using her as a scapegoat, so they believe they're still a few steps ahead of us."

They might not be that far ahead, but at least we have an advantage over them. I count the blessings. Do I feel bad for all the bad press that Coco is facing? No. It's because of her that we're in the middle of this mess.

"How long do you think she'll be in jail?"

"We hope it's until we're able to wrap this case or, if not, until we're far enough from Seattle and the Z's begin to attack us."

"You're expecting them to attack us?" she almost screeches.

"Yes, or we won't be able to fight them. Remember that tale of the Pied Piper of Hamelin?"

She shivers.

"Are you okay?"

"It's a little unsettling to think we'll be chased by rats. I hate rodents."

"I thought you loved bunnies."

"There's a big misconception about them. They're not rodents. They're part of the Leporidae family. I wouldn't mind being chased by a group of fluffy rabbits. These men are not that."

"We can't go back, but if you want to call it quits…" I trail my voice as I make my way onto I-5.

"No, I'm staying. We're doing this."

"That's my girl."

"I. Am. Not. Your. Girl." She clears her throat and says, "During the duration of the mission, we're not going to be anything to each other. Probably partners in crime, but nothing more. *Capisce?*"

"*Capisce,*" I say, but I might steal a kiss or two to keep me motivated.

Chapter Twenty-Four

Seth

RAW ENERGY HUMS through me as we head down to Oregon. I glance at my dashboard. There are no messages. Then to the rearview mirror. So far, it doesn't look like we're being followed. But looks can be deceiving.

Teddy sits quietly next to me. Hands on her lap and, I guess, eyes on the road. That's very uncharacteristic of her. She's always either chatting or arguing with me about one thing or another. Not today. It's as if we're heading to a funeral or something.

The thought of that reminds me of Pipe. The life of the party, one of the most giving people I've known. The boss, as Jude, Gabe, and I used to call her when we were young.

How are those two handling this? I couldn't even talk to Jude. Gabe doesn't want to think about it. He believes she's crafty enough to get away from whoever kidnapped her. I hope he's right. If we don't find her, I'll try to figure out what happened to her once this is over.

"Are we making any stops?" Teddy finally breaks the uncomfortable silence.

"We have everything we need in this car."

"Even a porta potty?" She sneers. "I don't plan on peeing in a cup."

I can't help but burst into laughter. "Who pees in a cup while driving?"

"People who drive for a living and can't take breaks. This is something serious, not some joke one of my brothers cracked. I had a long talk with them to ensure they're giving their employees breaks. It's a human right. Though, I watched *Cobra Kai...* and Johnny peed in bottles to save time while working as a driver and a food delivery boy."

"Most likely a way to bring some awareness, but not the point. I will stop if you need it unless we're being followed."

"Are we?"

"I don't think so."

What else can I tell her? They can track us in many other ways. Even though I swept the car, ensuring that there're no bugs, now I want to change vehicles. I'm tempted to stop by

Beacon's cabin in Oregon, but what if I attract the wrong people to his hometown? I don't think his brothers or my father would be happy about it.

No, I'll stick with the plan. We have a twenty-hour drive to San Diego, where we'll take a break. Then, we'll take a boat to Baja and grab the second car in Sonora, Mexico. That could give the teams in South America enough time to find the cell.

"You wouldn't tell me if they were right behind us. I think we have to establish some kind of trust between us."

"I thought we had already done that."

"No. I trust you with my life, but will you entrust me with what's happening around us? I want to know what you're thinking."

Oh, but she doesn't want to know that at all.

Right now, my mind is split between two main subjects. The mission and her. Mostly her and her scent. It's hard to control myself when I have this sexy beautiful woman just a few inches away from me. Do I want to run my hands through her soft brown hair? I'm dying to do it. I could combust with lust.

It's always been a challenge to keep my distance from her, and now, because of karma, Teddy is sitting next to me during one of the most important missions I've done in my entire career.

That's not karma, asshole, it was your fault for leaving people behind. Damn it. I have to push aside the guilt and my desires. *Concentrate on this mission.*

We can't lose anyone else. I have to trust myself and trust that I'll keep Teddy alive. Seeing the raw fear in her eyes when she was in the ambulance haunts me. I want to erase everything she's lived through because of me, and I doubt I'll ever be able to make it up to her.

"Why are you always brooding?"

"Excuse me?" I don't understand what she's asking.

"I tell you something, and you brood." She snorts. "You remind me of those car commercials where Matthew McConaughey has this look like he smelled something rotten and is looking at the horizon hoping that someone will fix the issue for him."

She pauses. I can see in the corner of my eye she's glancing at her hand. "He's too pretty and his car is too cool for him to fix the problem himself. But in the meantime, he has some existential monologue playing in the background."

I can't help but burst into laughter.

"I don't think I can be a brooding cowboy. Unless you're telling me I'm too pretty and calling my car cool." I turn to look at her and wink before looking back at the road. "Which one is it?"

"He's not a brooding cowboy," she corrects me. "We're not discussing him but your eternal silence."

"So we established that I'm pretty," I tease her.

"No. It's your silence."

I grin. "Maybe I like to hear you talk."

"No, because when it's time to antagonize me, argue, or tease me, you're pretty vocal."

I grin. "Mom always says I'm like Dad. He only speaks when it's necessary."

"Well, let me tell you it is not necessary to give me a hard time."

"I'd like to *argue* that point."

She groans. "You're annoying."

"Annoying, huh?" I pretend to pout. "And here I thought you were finally telling me how pretty and cool I am."

"I can't deal with you."

The advantage of having a sister is that I learned at a young age to give her a hard time to distract her. It's pretty easy to upset Grace and make her forget a grudge, or that she's running late, or that maybe my father was too overprotective.

It's a good tool to use with Teddy. Not because I want to upset her but because it distracts her from whatever is happening around us. In this case, the mission.

"We might be stuck in the car for weeks. Are you sure you're up to the challenge?"

"What is this challenge?"

"I don't know. Maybe I'm talking out loud, telling myself that I might not survive this trip. You sound so annoyed, I fear for my life."

She chuckles. "If you ask me nicely, I might spare your life. But you'll have to behave and give me more information than you give me."

But how much can I give her without her going into panic mode?

Chapter Twenty-Five

Teddy

I SMOOTH my hands down my lap. It's been hours. Okay, a little more than three, and we haven't stopped. We passed Portland, which I hadn't visited in years. The only times I've been there is when Fletcher invites me to go to a hockey game. He believes in supporting the Orcas hockey team, even though the ownership changed, and they now play in Portland.

"Do you know what will be more fun?"

"Please don't say if we had music," Seth says.

"What do you have against music?"

"Have you met my family?"

I can't help but laugh. "Everyone is very talented. I don't understand why you don't play an instrument. Even Archer played piano."

"You can blame Piper for your brother's flaws."

We fall silent after he mentions her, but I break it by saying, "She was calm."

"Calm?"

"It's weird to explain, but yes. She didn't sound panicked or… it's like she was expecting it."

Seth swerves before parking on the shoulder. His attention is on me. "What do you mean she was calm?"

"Yes. She acted as though nothing was happening. As if it'd go away. Even when she urged me to leave."

He presses the bridge of his nose. "That doesn't make sense."

I shrug. "As time passes, I remember more of what happened during the attack. Like the things she said, 'It's okay.' Also, something like, 'It'll be fine, Teddy.' Oh, and she also added at some point, 'He's here to protect us.'"

"What else did she say?"

"That's all I remember, but if anything comes to mind, I'll tell you more. She probably thought our bodyguard would do his job. Who knew he was already dead?"

"But she tried to fight?"

"Yes, I remember that too. Maybe she did run."

He nods a couple of times and pulls out his phone. "I'm

going to text Nathan a couple of places where she might be hiding."

"I thought you guys looked everywhere."

"Yes, but not in our usual hiding spots. We're searching with the assumption that someone took her away. Maybe she hid and hasn't reached out to us because she's injured."

My back relaxes slightly. "That's probably why she was calm, wasn't it? She knew what to do."

"With four little siblings and a bunch of cousins, she learned to look chill even when she was anxious. She likes to make everyone feel good about themselves or safe," he blurts. "She was probably hurt but was able to escape."

"That's good, isn't it?"

"Yes."

"I hope they find her in time."

"They will," he says reassuringly. "So what would make this trip more fun?"

"If we had a schedule of places we could visit."

"It's not a road trip, Theodora."

"But wouldn't it be amazing?"

"You sound like a child who's never been on vacation and is hoping someone will take pity on her."

I've gone on vacation plenty of times. I've traveled around the world with my family, but never in a car. Never. It's always in private jets and exclusive limos. Everything else is beneath my father. I adore the man, but he's a snob.

"Have you gone on a road trip?" Seth's voice sounds curious.

"Of course. Mom and I drove from Paris to Italy during my twenty-first birthday." I don't add that we had a driver.

"When this is over, I'll take you on a real road trip so you can have the whole experience."

"As I said, I've done it."

He chuckles. "A European road trip with your snooty family doesn't count."

"It does."

"Nope. You have to experience the States. The famous holes-in-the-wall the cities have to offer. There's food you can't taste at five-star restaurants."

"Your family has money too."

"They do, but there's a difference between your parents and mine. My family is well off but also down to earth. The St. Jameses, well…"

"We are not—"

"See, I have to stop you right there. I lived with two of your brothers for six years. Let me tell you, it was an experience. Mom flew to Boston to teach Zach and Burke how to cook. You have butlers and cooks and… Your parents live in a different reality."

I hate to admit that he's right. If it weren't for my brothers, I would be a totally different person. Love the 'rents, but their idea of slumming it during vacation is not having people catering to all their needs twenty-four seven.

"Sorry, I didn't mean to insult them. They're good people."

"I'm not upset about your comment, but at Mom and Dad." I hate to admit it to Seth, but I add, "You're right. They're out of touch with the world. Did I tell you Mom almost gave Matilda a diet book for her birthday? My niece is just a kid, why bother her with weight management at this or any age? It wasn't done with bad intentions. She was taught at an early age that girls have to maintain a certain weight."

"That's terrible. Please tell me she didn't do it with you."

"Oh, but she did. It was a struggle. After years of therapy, I've learned to love myself and not care about looking like a toothpick for someone to love me."

His hand squeezes mine. "You're beautiful. You know that, right?"

"Thank you," I say, because if there's someone who makes me feel good about myself, it's Seth.

Though he rejects me because of his guilt, he always tells me how gorgeous I am when we fuck. After this trip, we have to stop doing whatever we've done for so many years. I really appreciate what he's done for me. I won't be able to put it into words.

He's been there for me when the sadness of losing my brother pulls me down into the hellhole. Those days I feel lost and can't wrap my head around what I need to do to take another step. He's the only one who knows about it. My brothers are amazing, but I have difficulty trusting them with my feelings.

"I'm telling you the truth. You're one of the most beautiful women I've met." His phone buzzes, and he chuckles.

"What?"

He shakes his head.

"I thought we agreed that we would trust each other."

"Beacon texted me to keep moving and stop making out in

the car." Seth's pale gray eyes stare at me, deep inside me. They always seem to know what I'm thinking or what I'm feeling.

I hate that it's hard to hide from him and that no one else in the world can make things better the way he does. Which is ironic because sometimes he's the one person who makes me feel at my worst.

For the next few days or weeks, I just need to be careful not to touch him or melt into his arms when he's close by. I can manage to avoid him, and after, I could try therapy to forget him. I wish there was a way to erase him and everything that's happened between us. All of it.

But can my heart forget him?

Chapter Twenty-Six

Seth

ACCORDING to Beacon and his team, no one has followed us so far. He suggests I stop in Eugene and treat this like a road trip instead of an escape. See if that makes the cartel believe our guard is down, and they attack us.

To no one's surprise, except maybe Beacon's, I say hell no and continue driving. I hate to wait, but I do at least slow down my pace, just in case there's someone behind who has to catch up.

I ask if we can stop somewhere more touristy, like Portland or Baker's Creek. I wouldn't mind driving back to those places. At least I would know what to do, and there's some backup there in case we get into trouble.

Teddy would enjoy it since it looks like she's never been out on a real vacation. She might say she has, but I know her brothers. During our family vacations, we were allowed to bring a friend. Since I was eight, I brought Archer along. He always said he had more fun with us than with his parents. Once Archer was old enough to take his siblings on vacation, he ditched his parents and took his brothers.

He only did that with Teddy once, during our trip to Vegas. We know how that turned out.

It takes about an hour before I get a call from Beacon.

"Yeah," I answer, parking on the shoulder and leaving the car, so Teddy doesn't listen to the conversation.

"You're not going to like this," he says.

"Of course not, but you're still going to say something stupid that I'll hate. You might even try to convince me to do it. Spit it out."

"We opened a few social media accounts for Teddy."

"Doesn't she have her own?"

"Yes, but they're private, and under a funny name that only her friends and family know."

It's not funny, but I won't argue with him. "Okay, so you opened this account for what?"

"We're setting them up so it looks like they've been there for a few months. Our team is photoshopping some pictures of the two of you as we speak. They'll add them with corny captions. We'll also post pictures about the road trip."

I tap my lips with my index finger. "How is that going to help us?"

"We're sending it to those gossip sites that Coco used to get exposure. They'll probably make a big fuss about it."

My chest tightens at the thought of what this could do to Teddy. I want to slam my hand on the car, yell at Beacon, or... I calm myself down, remembering that I have to trust him and the team. "Why are we doing this?"

"So they know where to follow you because we're so far away and no one is behind you."

I thread my fingers through my hair, trying not to scream. This can't be happening. "Why is that?"

"Our theory is that they might be regrouping or finding a way to get to you. We're making it easier for you and faster for us."

I pace back and forth. "Is Dad okay with your plan?"

"He's following our lead and only said that you have to be okay with it before it begins."

I cock a brow, wondering if they tied him to a chair so they could do whatever the fuck they wanted. This is so unlike my father. "That sounds dangerous."

"The plan?"

"That too, but I mean my father not giving any input."

"I think he's testing us," he whispers. "I feel like I'm in the middle of an exam, and if we fail..."

"We all die?" I finish for him.

"There's that, but I don't mean that kind of failure. More like, if he believes I'm fucking up, he'll replace me and take charge of the operation. Then, he'll never let me lead a mission ever again."

"Oh, that is a weird thought, but it makes sense."

"Enough about my current issue. I'm going to send you the login for the new social media accounts. We need you to start posting fun pictures of the two of you enjoying this romantic trip."

"It's not—"

"Can you pretend, please? Imagine this is an undercover mission, and you have to act like her doted-on boyfriend... or are you the one doing the doting? It doesn't matter. Look like you're madly in love, have her take the pictures and post them. Food, places, kisses..."

Kisses? Is he kidding me?

It's so hard to avoid having any contact with her, and he wants me to kiss her? We should've used a decoy or brought a chaperone with us. If our lips touch, I won't let her go. It's going to be impossible to move away from her.

"You should've consulted with me before making that decision. What you're asking is for us to be real sitting ducks."

"Yes. Also, I'm sending you the itinerary of your trip."

"What do you mean an itinerary? This is insane."

"Believe me, I know, and I'm not thrilled about this turn of events. However, unless we can find the cartel hiding in South America, this is our only lead."

"It's not a lead."

"But it is," he argues. "They want you."

"Dead. They want me dead."

"Understandable, but you shouldn't worry about it. We'll do everything possible to ensure you come out of this alive."

"I hate you."

"Ah, there it is. You Bradleys have such a special way of letting me know how much I mean to you."

After hanging up, I open the car's door and stare at Teddy.

"Is everything okay?" She grins at me.

"Your wish just came true."

She bites her bottom lip while arching her eyebrow. She's so fucking adorable I want to kiss her. Instead of jumping her, I hold onto the door tightly while thinking of hockey statistics and the next board meeting for my company. Once I regain control of myself, I get inside the car and say, "We're going on an official road trip."

"Does this mean we're out of danger?"

"No. It means we're going to look like two people having fun while we wait for someone to attack us."

She sucks in a ragged breath. "You're kidding."

"I wish." I laugh humorlessly. "We failed to drag anyone along with us, so now we have to make a bigger fuss about this trip and wait."

"Where are we going?"

I shake my phone. "Waiting for orders."

"Your dad is sending us on a road trip?" There's some enthusiasm in her voice, but I have to shut her down.

"Nope. Beacon is the one who had this fantastic idea." I can see it already. We're going to attract the wrong crowd, and we'll be hiding from all of them while Beacon's team slowly gets rid of them.

When this ends, we'll be having a few words.

No, a lot.

Chapter Twenty-Seven

Teddy

WE END the day in a small town called Happy Springs. It's close to Mt. Hood. We have dinner at a fancy restaurant that's close to the bed-and-breakfast where we'll be spending the night.

The food is delicious, and the atmosphere is pleasant.

We're on the terrace, close to the fireplace, enjoying a nice bottle of wine with our meal. This is the first time I'm having dinner with Seth. Only the two of us, without our families and the excuse of a holiday, a birthday, or our monthly get-together with the Deckers because our families are close.

In a way, this is supposed to be a date. I already took pictures of the table, and I'll take one of us once we're done. I'll post them on all my new social media accounts with some captions that'll make everyone envious of my extraordinary life and my handsome husband.

Everything is a lie, though. We've never been together like this. And how I wish we could've at least gone out on one date. There's no point in rehashing our past and the terrible habit we have of fucking each other's brains out while meaning nothing to each other.

Sure, he says I'm one of the most important people in his life, but that's probably the biggest lie he's ever told.

"Are you okay?" Seth asks, pointing at the bottle of wine.

I nod. I'm peachy. This is my first date with Seth Bradley and it's not real.

I'm a lucky girl.

"So that cabin where we switched cars is part of the safe houses The Organization owns?"

Seth shakes his head as he pours wine into my glass. "It's owned by a friend."

"Cryptic."

He looks around and leans closer. "Remember those times when you visit your mother's town and avoid discussing certain subjects in public?"

I smile, understanding immediately what he means. In many small towns, people have great hearing and like to spread rumors like wildfire. Even though no one knows us, it's best if we don't mention anything about what we're doing.

"I love Silver Lake. Did I tell you Mom wants to sell the house and downsize?"

"I'm guessing you don't want to lose it?"

"No. It's where we grew up. I'd love to keep it and make it the vacation home for the St. James family. We could add a pool and share it with friends—even with your family."

He touches his heart. "Even? I thought we were closer than that."

"Keep the dramatics to yourself. I won't believe that you're suffering in any way."

"So you're buying the house," he prompts me to continue.

"Well, no. It's pretty expensive, and I doubt she'll give it to me at a discount. I'm still paying for…" I clamp my mouth and let out a breath.

"What happened?"

I lean closer to him and whisper, "I don't have a condo anymore."

"Who's taking care of the insurance?" His voice is low, and our bodies are close. So close, I almost burn with his heat. How are we going to spend the night together in a room without having sex?

I don't remember why we shouldn't have sex. All I can think of is his smoldering eyes and that gravelly voice.

"Teddy, the insurance?" He brings me back from my almost naughty thoughts.

"King offered to take care of it. They'll probably pay the mortgage company, give me a little for the assets I had in the property. How about yourself? Burke mentioned your penthouse exploded or something like that."

He nods a couple of times. "It was controlled, so there's not much damage to the property."

"How about your belongings?"

"Once they repair the water and smoke damage, I'll buy new furniture."

"And the rest?"

"I don't understand?"

"All my things are gone. Clothes, pictures, souvenirs... I assume the same happened with you."

He rolls his eyes. "I'm practical. Everything that matters is in a safe or at my parents' house."

"Or in your museum?" I snap my fingers. "Right, you don't save anything in there."

"I don't save anything at all. My apartment was almost identical to the house you visited last week."

"You need an intervention."

He shakes his head and checks his watch. "Why don't we call it a night? We have to be on the road tomorrow morning."

"Where are we going tomorrow?"

"San Francisco," he answers. "Ever been there?"

"During nerdy conventions, does that count?"

He laughs. "No. We'll be out and about. If I could drink on the job, I'd have taken you to wine country."

"It's okay, with my brother's vineyards, I can have all the wine I want."

When we arrive at the bed-and-breakfast, I change into my pajamas. I'm thankful that Aaron sent more than just sexy lingerie. I swear, the next time I see him, I will fire him. Whoever told him to get me some clothes forgot to remind him about common sense while choosing the items.

"How are we doing this?" I ask when I come out of the bathroom.

Seth is already pulling the pillows from the bed.

"I'm sleeping on the floor," he says.

"That's crazy. We're two adults who can share—"

"A full-size bed is too small for me. I don't think it's a good idea to share it."

"We could add some pillows."

"Theodora, I appreciate your effort, but no. I'll take the floor."

"It's uncomfortable."

"I've slept in more uncomfortable places than the plush carpet of this room."

"But I feel bad about letting you…"

His eyes darken, and his jaw clenches. Is he upset with me?

"Take your anger somewhere else," I warn him.

Seth laughs. "Anger? No, sweetheart. This is me trying to control my body because I want you. No. I *need* you under me. If you keep offering your bed, I'm going to take it and then take you."

I gasp.

"Exactly. So do us a favor and stop insisting on where I should sleep. If I touch you, I won't be able to stop myself."

"I'll never understand you."

"What's there to understand, Teddy?"

"Why you want me, and yet you reject me."

He rubs his chin a couple of times. "That's something I've been asking myself. I might get a few answers during our trip."

"Answers about?"

"Us. If you recall, ten years ago, I vowed to love and protect you for the rest of our lives. What happens after the vows? Usually, there's a marriage, and with us…"

"It was something silly."

"That weekend wasn't silly, Theodora. It mattered to me. My friends joke that I lost my virginity at twenty-one. Do you know why?"

I shake my head.

"You're the only person who's mattered to me. I only count you. My sister swears I must sleep around with randoms because I don't have the time. Ever since I was twenty-one, you've been my random. But that's not who you are."

He walks toward his bag, pulls out some clothes, and before he goes into the bathroom, he says, "I need to understand what you are to me because you're too fucking important to keep messing with your heart and my head."

Chapter Twenty-Eight

Teddy

THE AROMA of coffee forces me to open my eyes. I inhale deeply before pushing the blankets down and swinging my legs off the bed. Seth is no longer on the floor, but his pillow remains there. I feel bad for not insisting he sleep on the bed with me.

But maybe he's right. We're not going back to screwing with each other's minds. Well, that's not what he said—more like he's done messing with my heart. At least he's aware of what he's been doing to me, but have I done the same to him?

After we finish having sex, we both get defensive and lash out at each other.

He wants to figure out what I mean to him. Should I do the same? Since we signed the divorce papers, I've been trying to avoid thinking about the fact we got married in Vegas and that in just a few months, it'll be over. Over, even though it never really started.

We need to talk more about our screwed-up relationship and what makes us behave like we do. The biggest problem might be Seth and his lack of communication skills. He's a smart man, but he doesn't talk much. I wasn't lying when I said the only time he talks is to tease me or antagonize me.

Seth Bradley is a man of action. When he's the most frustrated, he kisses me as if he wants me to soothe him or make everything better. I should stop thinking about him. I dig my toes into the soft carpet, stretching my arms high, wanting to touch the ceiling. When I walk toward the bathroom, I spot a mug and a note next to it.

I had to check on a few things. You're safe in the B&B. I'll be back as soon as I'm done.

SB

P.S. Enjoy the latte. There's a pastry in the bag.

Warmth flares deep in my chest as I find a cheese muffin inside the paper bag. He remembered me mentioning that it sounded delicious. I break off a piece and pop it into my mouth. A moan escapes me right when the door opens. It's Seth, wearing a pair of dark jeans and a black t-shirt. I freeze, feeling like I should be ready to leave and realizing I slept through the night and didn't have a single nightmare.

"Good morning," he greets me, his gaze raking over me from head to toe.

I resist the urge to toss my arms around his neck and beg him to take me. "Thank you," I mumble. My voice is all low and husky from just waking up. I clear my throat. "Sorry, I just woke up. If you give me a minute, I'll be ready."

"Did you sleep alright?" he asks as I take another bite of my muffin and wash it down with the almost cold latte. "How long were you gone?"

"A few hours." I check the clock on the wall, and it's just seven in the morning.

"Did you sleep?"

"A few hours."

"Where did you go?"

"The team decided to spend the night close by. It seemed like a good idea to meet before we started the day."

"Any updates?"

"We're still going south. We'll try to stick to small towns."

"Any particular reason?"

"There are fewer people. It's easier to control the chaos if anything happens."

"How bad can this get?" I dare to ask.

His eyebrows rise. "What exactly do you want to know?"

"When I think about your job, I always wonder if you're a lot like double-o-seven, but sometimes it sounds more like an episode of *Jack Ryan*, if that makes any sense."

He snorts loudly. "That's pretty funny. Every mission is different."

"Are there explosions?"

"Yes, and we use our weapons. Not that we like to do it. Will there be explosions? Probably. But if things go as planned, you won't see anything."

I hug myself with one hand. "Other than the anxiety-induced fear? The tension in my shoulders and the stomach pain because I don't know what will happen or when?"

"There's that," he says.

"This is better, you know?" I say, glancing at my pajamas. "Well, not being in a room with you, but moving. It'd drive me crazy to be in a house just waiting. I don't know how my brothers are dealing with it. How long will they be off the grid?"

He shoves his hands in his pockets. "That's a hard question to answer. We're taking everything one day at a time."

"I feel like you have me in the dark."

He smirks. "Oh, baby, I wouldn't mind having you any way you want me to."

"That's not what I meant. What happened to not touching me until you solve your existential crisis?"

"I'm pretty sure that's not what I said."

"Same thing," I argue.

"I'll keep my promise." His gray eyes darken, turning the color of a stormy winter day as he scoots a fraction closer to me. "Unless you ask nicely. Then, I'll break the promise and do whatever you want me to do—in the dark."

"You are impossible." I place my cup on the table and head to the bathroom. "I'm taking a shower so we can leave. Keep your thoughts PG and your hands to yourself."

"Unless—"

I point a warning finger. "Say it, and you'll regret it."

"It's funny how many people fear me but never you."

I smirk. "Because I'm more powerful than anyone."

"You're the most frustrating woman I know. Not sure if that's a good power to have."

I shut the door, ignoring him. We have too many days together and figuring out our future shouldn't be done in just a couple of days.

Chapter Twenty-Nine

Teddy

"WE HAVE to stop by a store to buy clothes," I say, frustrated with my outfit.

From everything that Aaron packed me, this is the most modest dress I could find. He only sent dresses. I need pants. Not skirts that barely cover my butt cheeks. If I had my cell phone with me, I would be firing him right at this moment.

There won't be any severance package or letter of recommendation. What was he thinking? If we didn't have to take pictures during this pretend road trip and post them, I would be wearing the armor Grace gave me.

When I look up, my heart comes to a complete stop as I notice Seth is wearing nothing but a pair of boxer briefs that barely cover the bulge between his legs. My mouth waters, and it's hard to force my gaze upward, knowing exactly what's there and the things I would love to do to it—and his entire body.

He's all muscular, sharp lines, and tattoos.

His body is like Chris Evans's... or maybe Zac Efron's. Though his face is like Sean O'Pry's.

No.

He's all Seth Bradley.

Unique and delicious.

But I can't have him.

"Get dressed," I order, but I can't help but lick my lips, savoring him. I know his taste, his scent, and his body.

I'm aware of everything I'm missing because...

Why are we not supposed to get tangled up? There's a bed. Not that we need it. I just want to wrap my legs around him and have him push me—

"Stop looking at me like that." Seth's low voice makes me tremble.

I blink a couple of times as I fight back the words, *take me, please*. I push them down. Deep down so they never make it out again. He takes a couple of steps forward. I take one back. We're close.

So close.

His hand reaches out and tucks a strand of hair behind my ear, cupping the back of my neck.

"Theodora." The way he says my name, like a soft whisper to the wind. Like a wish that might come true.

His gaze zeroes in on my mouth as he leans closer and his lips part. I'm at a crossroads. This is the moment when I have to pull away and run or meet him. I want his lips so much. I've been needing them since this mess began and now... Now, I'm burning for him.

"Stop me," he mutters, but I don't listen. I stretch my neck and meet his lips.

The kiss is soft at first. Gentle. Like a feather moving with the wind, until the pace changes and he grips my neck, coaxing my mouth to open and claiming it. I give in, demanding just as much as he does. It's a hungry kiss, but also desperate. There's a feeling I've never felt. It's more than the usual need. There's a fear of this being the last time. I clutch his shoulders, savoring this moment, praying it's not the last, wanting it to be the first.

First kisses are the best, and the first with him is forever seared in my mind.

When he pulls back, I whimper, almost begging for more. He kisses my jaw, feathering kisses along my neckline. "You drive me crazy," he says.

"Is that what you've been thinking all along? This woman drives me crazy, I must kiss her?"

"Don't taunt me, minx. I can't get enough of you, but as I said yesterday, we can't just continue doing the same thing for the rest of our lives."

I open my mouth to say that I wouldn't care but something different escapes. "Rest of our lives? You didn't plan on settling?

Just have Teddy on the side when it pleases you?" My voice is loud and angry.

Is he fucking kidding me?

"No. That's not what I meant."

I cross my arms. "By all means, what did you mean by that?"

He stares at my chest, closes his eyes, and shakes his head. "You look amazing, but do you happen to have a sweater or something to cover you? I won't be able to drive comfortably with a permanent hard-on."

"As I said, I need to buy clothes. Aaron didn't choose the right garments for the trip." I wave a hand around his almost naked body. "How about you? I don't need to see your eight-pack and those bulging muscles."

He grins and winks. "You never complained about them before."

"If I have to abstain, I shouldn't be looking at them."

He begins to put on some clothes. "Sorry, I needed to change."

"You could've done it while I took a shower."

"I received a call from Beacon."

My heart stutters. The last time they talked, he switched the plan. "Is everything okay? You said you were in a meeting with them."

He waves a hand as if there's nothing significant to report.

"You have to be honest with me."

"They think someone might've taken the bait. They made a post on your behalf saying we're heading to Eugene, Oregon."

"I thought we were stopping in San Fran."

"We want to try a shorter drive."

"Okay, but please, let's stop at a store. I need something less revealing."

"Only if we make a deal."

Anything for a pair of leggings and a comfortable top. "What is that?"

He wiggles his eyebrows. "Once this is over, we take another road trip, and you wear that dress and all the lingerie Aaron sent."

"How do you know about it?"

He points at my luggage, where I can see all the lacy items my assistant dared to send me. "I can see it from here."

Heat creeps all the way to the tip of my hair. "That's..." He's insane if he thinks I'll be wearing that for him.

"You want new clothes or not?"

I huff. "Fine."

He grins like a child who just got promised candy after dinner. What Seth doesn't know is that I won't be taking that trip. I'm taking this as a self-discovery journey where I'll figure out the main reason why I shouldn't be with him again.

Chapter Thirty

Teddy

INSTEAD OF DRIVING BACK to Portland, Vance Aldridge, Beacon's brother, flies us in his helicopter. I had no idea he works for The Organization. I guess everything stays in the family. Seth or someone he knows gets us access to the shopping mall so I can shop early.

I post several pictures of the outfits Teddy would buy if she was going on a road trip with her husband. I, on the other hand, buy comfortable clothing for this trip. Even my underwear is cotton with cute decorations. No thongs with lace that sticks up my ass. Since I don't have money with me, Seth pays. It makes me feel very *Pretty Woman* since he also includes all the outfits that looked good on me but are impractical.

"You didn't model any of those clothes for me," Seth says in a flirty tone.

I nudge him with my hip. "We're not supposed to be flirting, remember?"

"Sex. We said no sex," he clarifies.

"Flirting is the prelude to sex."

He snorts. "Says who?"

"I don't know. It must be in some manual."

"A manual?" His voice is filled with curiosity. "I would believe it more if it were a book."

"Yes, of course. It's a self-help book called 'How To Get Over Your Annoying Ex-husband, When You Never Dated.' Step one is dating him until you realize he's not worth it. It's like a twelve-step program."

He puts an arm around my shoulders and kisses my temple. "Are you complaining that we never dated? I could take you wherever you want. Italy for pizza. Mexico for tacos. There's always Paris. We can have dinner on top of the Eiffel Tower."

"Who takes anyone on those kinds of dates? That's insane."

"Grandpa Chris took my grandfather on those dates." He pauses, looking at me a little offended before he smiles. "And he is a little crazy."

His maternal grandfathers are the cutest couple I've ever met. Every time I hear a story about them, I melt. That's exactly what I want in a man. Someone who'll do crazy things for me—even tacos in Mexico.

"So, if I take you on a date, will I be allowed to flirt with you?"

"No. It's not about dating or... I meant to say that we were nothing. The marriage happened because my brother—may he rest in peace—pranked you at my expense."

"If you recall, he thought we'd be great together."

"We're talking about a man who, after his first day of preschool, came home and told Mom he met his wife. Archer was a fool."

"The jury is still out on that one. I think he was a misunderstood man with a brilliant plan. Yes, he did crazy things for Piper." He stiffens and looks around the parking lot.

The hair on the back of my neck stands up. "What's wrong?"

"Nothing. I thought about crazy Archer," he says dismissively. "Well, crazy but a visionary." Seth's voice loses the humor it had before.

I want to believe that he's thinking about my brother and his antics, so I continue with the conversation, hoping there's nothing wrong. "You can't tell me that what he did was smart."

He opens the trunk to shove the shopping bags in when his jaw tenses. "Get inside the SUV right now," he orders before he pushes me into the trunk. The door shuts as a car screeches to a stop, and I hear the gunfire around me. I cover my ears, praying that nothing happens to Seth.

There's the sound of the door opening. My heart pounds loudly in my ears. I want to shout, ask what's happening. The

186 • CLAUDIA BURGOA

engine comes to life. "Don't move. I'll get us out of here in a second.

"Where are you, Beacon?" I hear him say, the car pulling out of its parking spot.

"What's happening?" I hear a voice through the speakers.

"As you might've seen, they attacked us outside the shopping center."

"I'm glad you went before it opened. There won't be any casualties."

"Where are you?"

"Arriving at the scene. We caught one alive. We'll be interrogating him. How did you kill this many and escape?"

"I don't think I eliminated more than one. I thought you were there, helping me."

Beacon says something I can't hear before saying, "We're sweeping the area. I'll keep you updated with more information soon."

"Where should we head now?"

"Eugene. Continue the trip as we agreed. We'll have someone meet you halfway to exchange vehicles."

"Call if anything changes," Seth says before ending the call. "Are you okay, Teddy?"

No. How can he expect me to be okay when we almost died? I don't say any of that out loud though.

"Can I take a seat now?"

"Yes, sorry about that."

I crawl out of the trunk and onto the middle bench. "Did they hurt you?"

"Everything is fine." He's calm. Unemotional. I don't

understand how that didn't affect him. My heart continues beating at a thousand miles per hour.

"How can you say that? We were almost killed!" Every cell of my body is shaking.

Nausea rolls up my stomach as I move toward the front, and I puke my breakfast on the seat.

"I guess I'll stay back here." I sit on the second-row bench, securing my seat belt.

"Definitely not okay," he says. "We're alive, baby. I told you nothing would happen, and I keep my promises."

I nod, wanting to be okay. He's fine. I'm alive, but something triggers the tears.

I can't suck it up the way he does.

My life passed before my eyes in seconds. No. It wasn't my life but the worry of what could've happened to Seth.

What if he had been shot?

Or killed.

Hot tears spill down my cheeks. I don't know if I can do this. I don't know if I can keep going until The Organization traps them.

I want him to stop the car and send me somewhere safe— with him. Knowing he'd stay on the road until it was over, I decide to be with him.

We will go down together, but I hope neither one of us goes down.

Chapter Thirty-One

Seth

TEDDY'S TREMBLING and crying in the back seat. I want to stop this mission but it's impossible. We could lose a lot if we don't put a stop to the cartel. This ambush... Beacon's plan worked perfectly. I should've known they could be anywhere nearby and been prepared, but yet, I knew we were in the eye of the storm about to face a tornado of bullets.

Something happened in the parking lot, I just can't figure

out what alerted me. That gut feeling I usually get when I'm on a mission and my people are watching over me, hit me. The low buzz took over, setting me into survivor mode. If it hadn't been for that, we wouldn't have made it out alive.

Something about the scene doesn't add up and I hope Dad or Beacon has answers. I was able to get my gun out, probably shot a few men and might've killed one. The way Beacon described it though, that I finished them all? That's impossible. Not when my main goal was to escape so I could keep Teddy safe.

Someone wanted her dead. My stomach twists every time I think of what can happen to Teddy if we continue on this road, but also what will happen if I don't finish everyone who knows about her. I have to keep the lid on my emotions, but I need a break before we get back on the road.

Gripping the wheel tightly, I take a sharp U-turn on the next street. Instead of taking I-5 and continuing our trip, I drive toward The Organization's hangar. They can fly us to our next destination. No one knows where we're at, and they won't have a clue until we begin to post again.

"Where are we going?" Teddy's voice comes out like a mumble.

"Change of plans," I say, dialing Dad's phone but then disconnecting and calling Beacon. He's in charge of this operation, and I won't undermine his authority.

If he's right and Dad is testing him, I won't be the one fucking things up for him. He could be another person being invited to be a part of the A team.

"Yeah?" Beacon answers right away.

"I'm flying to San Fran."

"W-why the sudden change?"

I need a break? How will he take it if I tell him something like that? I prefer not to say out loud that we need to recharge before we continue this crazy chase.

Instead of answering, I ask, "No one knows where we're going until we post on social media, right?"

"Yes. These men arrived in Portland after we let the world know you were here, taking time off with your girl. Nathan is running plates, the private jet, and the credit cards they have on them. We're guessing that after Teddy posted about your shopping spree, they decided to wait for you."

"Which means they don't know where in the world I'm hiding."

He whistles. "No one knows what happened to you since all the men are dead."

"That wasn't me."

"You said that, and we're looking into it."

I drum my fingers against the wheel. "Something isn't adding up. There's a team ahead of you—and right behind me."

"I don't believe they're our enemies."

"It's more like the enemy of my enemy is my friend," I say, trying to figure out if there's a second cartel involved.

"You're right, but what do we do? Do you have any ideas where to look?"

"There's nothing we can do. They haven't left any trace. Tell Nathan to hack into the CCTV."

"He already did that, and the same thing that happened in Seattle happened here. There's a chunk of footage replaced."

Who can be smart enough to be behind this? "Does The Organization have a competitor?" I ask out loud and then add, "Nathan can ask his underground forum. Hire a mercenary to do that kind of job. They might know the guy or guys."

"Do we want to look into it?"

"We need to figure out who they are. I wouldn't mind if suddenly we have competitors. But what if after we're done with the cartel, they decide we're no longer useful? They know how we operate and where to find us—all of us."

"I see your point. Do you need anything in San Fran?"

"Yes, a safe house ready to take us for the day. We'll get back on the road tomorrow, unless you need me to start before that."

"Sit tight, we'll be looking into the leads and call you if we have any news. In the meantime, rest. How's Teddy doing?"

"She's shaken."

"I'm fine." Her voice still trembles, but I don't argue with her.

But then I glance at the front seat. "Fine isn't the word I would use to describe your current condition." I reach for the glove compartment and give her the first aid kit we have in there. It includes wipes and even some toothpaste.

She takes it and says, "It's my first time. Puking should be allowed."

"It's part of the training," Beacon jokes. "Puke 101. She's ready for the next step."

"Can you get someone to detail this car?" I ignore his nonsense.

"Will do. Call us if you need anything, okay?"

"Thank you," Teddy says after Beacon hangs up and while she's cleaning herself and using the toothpaste.

"For?"

"Taking a break from the road trip of doom. I want to continue, but this was too intense."

When I park, I jump out of the car and open the passenger door. Teddy glances up, and when she stares at me, the vulnerability in her eyes feels like a punch to the gut. She takes off her seat belt, and I pull her into a tight hug.

Her arms wrap around me, holding me tightly.

Her head rests on my chest.

I can feel her rapid heartbeat.

I could get lost in this moment and never let her go.

Mine.

Untouchable.

I squeeze her tight. "Sorry for letting this happen to you."

"You couldn't have known this would happen."

"Still—" I slide my hands down her back as I lean down, devouring her mouth.

We don't speak, but we say everything with this kiss. I let all the fear of almost losing her run wild along with my tongue. I want to possess her just because I can have another day with her. A chance to have her. She rocks her hips against mine. She wants me just like I do, but I stop us.

This isn't the place to do it, nor the time. I should probably be the one piloting the plane. This might not be the best time to have sex with Teddy. I don't want it to be just because there's a lot of adrenaline running through my veins—and hers.

If this ever happens again, it's because she wants to give herself to me, not because we're afraid to lose each other.

But will that ever happen?

Chapter Thirty-Two

Teddy

I ALWAYS KNEW that being with Seth Bradley would be exciting and dangerous. What I expected was sex against a balcony, not automatic weapons being aimed at me. This is exactly why I should never date a man like him. Ever.

Now that I've had a taste of what being a part of The Organization means, I wonder why so many people work for them. I couldn't last with them more than a day. If it was possible, I would quit. Not that I can. We're in this together. I just need him to give me a few pointers on what to do the next time we're being targeted. Crying, running like a maniac, and rolling into a fetal position don't seem to be the best ways to help—or stay alive—during the situation.

Unfortunately, I can't ask any of that since he decides to pilot the jet that takes us to San Francisco. It's probably for the best. I can't have him see me losing my shit for what feels like the millionth time in the past week. This isn't me. I might've been sheltered by Donovan and Florence St. James, but I was raised by my brothers to be a strong and independent woman.

I don't have a weak stomach and I can handle pressure, but this is above my tolerance threshold.

Not even Archer tried to train me to escape psychos and trained assassins. If only my brother was around, I think everything would be a lot less crazy and simpler. He wouldn't have lost Piper. My stomach gets queasy just thinking about her.

When we land, I almost kiss the floor. Not because Seth is a bad pilot. It's because for the next day I'm free. I don't have to run or worry about anything. Also, I'm physically and emotionally exhausted. I could use a long shower and a nap.

Not surprisingly, there's a black SUV waiting for us.

"Do you guys get any other color of vehicles? It's either black or white, why?"

Seth smirks as he loads the trunk with our bags. So far, I haven't seen him carry a weapon, yet earlier one appeared from somewhere in the vehicle and he began to use it. I should ask where to find one. I might not know how to fight, but Archer did teach me to shoot. He said it was like an insurance policy. You hope you never use it, but it's good to have it.

"I hate to sound like a broken record, but are you okay?" Seth asks as he helps me into the SUV.

Mom always taught me to be polite even if I don't have anything good to say. "As good as I can be after having such an… interesting day."

"That's one way to describe it," he scoffs.

"How can you do this every day?"

"We don't do it every day, but when we do it, it's a matter of putting things into perspective. If I don't get it done, the world won't be a better place for others. It's for the greater good."

That's what Archer used to say. If you can at least save one life, one town... you make this world a better place. He and Seth were a lot alike but also different. That's why they were like brothers.

"When we arrive at the house, you can take a shower while I cook us something for lunch."

"Can I ask you a question?"

"Yeah?"

I wipe my hands on my jeans, nervous because this makes everything a million times more real. "If they kill you or we get separated—"

"It won't happen."

"But what if it does? I need to know what to do, don't you think?"

He's squeezing the steering wheel so hard his knuckles are white. "It can happen," I insist.

"Let me make a plan so you can follow it just in case," he says after a long pause. "We'll just try not to use it."

The rest of the drive is quiet. Not a calm, comfortable silence. There's tension, or maybe panic. He's probably thinking of how to ignore my request and do things his way.

We're staying in a small house in Presidio Heights. The house looks okay on the outside but pretty sad on the inside. I don't say anything and head to the room where I take a shower. When I come out, the smell of spices and fish invites me to head downstairs.

Seth's hair is still wet. He wears a pair of jeans and a t-shirt. No shoes. Even in this place he looks like he's at home.

"So you like to decorate your homes sterile-style?"

Glancing up at me from the stove, he arches an eyebrow. "What does that even mean?"

"There's nothing that says this is a home. You have one couch, a table, and two chairs." I wave a hand as if showing the poorly decorated area. "If you want, I know people who can help make this feel more homey."

Seth clenches his jaw. "We have beds too, but none of the safe houses are designed to welcome guests. They're temporary housing so our agents can take a break, or we can hide people who are on the run."

"Don't get snippy with me."

"I'm just pointing out that we don't need a decorator."

"Well, if I'm stuck here for days or weeks, I want it to feel less like I'm in *Orange is the New Black* and a little more like the set of *Friends*."

He rolls his eyes. "You're too sheltered."

"No one has ever said anything different. The only times I've camped outside my backyard were in the Deckers' back-yard when your cousin, Harper, invited me."

"I always forget you two are the same age." He serves the food and sets the plates on the table.

"I think your mother really wanted me to connect with her and be part of her group."

"Nah, if that had been her goal, you would still be close to Harp."

"She's nice, but it's different from you, Arch, and your cousins."

"Hey, I get it. No need to sound apologetic."

I shrug. "I feel like I failed your mother and she's such a nice lady."

He laughs. "Why would you say that?"

"She tried to pair me with many different people, and it never worked out."

"It's probably because you're different, but I'm sure that's not a problem. You were always more comfortable hanging out with adults during reunions and helping the hostess."

"How do you know?"

He shrugs. "I learned to observe my surroundings when I was young."

"Is that why you knew something was about to happen in the parking lot?"

He takes a seat at the table. "No, I just had that feeling. It's hard to explain to anyone. If Beacon can figure out exactly what happened, I might know."

"Okay." That doesn't sound reassuring, but there's nothing I can add to it.

"When we're out of here, I'm going to take you camping."

"Like with real tents and sleeping bags?" I try to sound like a spoiled socialite who's disgusted by the prospect, but I actually like the idea.

"Yep. I'll give you a taste of the real world."

I gulp at the sound of his sexy voice offering me a taste. There are so many things I want to try, but most of all, I want him.

Can I have him?

Chapter Thirty-Three

Teddy

"I'm thankful for the break, but what are we supposed to do when we can't go outside, use electronics unless it's an emergency, and there's no television?" I ask after washing the dishes from our lunch.

Seth's gray eyes darken. They are raw. Hungry.

He's ready to eat me, and without anything else to do in this house, I'm prepared for him to take me. We can try naked poker. Well, first, we'll have to play strip poker, but once the clothes are off, we can bet for sexual favors.

"Don't look at me like that," he warns in the low, dominant rasp that makes my body quiver.

"Or what?" I challenge him.

"We can't." He doesn't sound convinced at all. "You have to stop tempting me."

Why does it excite me? He makes it sound like he's all innocent, and I'm luring him into some kind of trap. Look who's talking. The guy who took my virginity and has shown me everything I know.

"Are you scared of little ol' me, Seth Bradley?"

"Be careful when playing with fire, you might get burned." His cautious voice makes my heart pound wildly in my chest.

"I'm not scared."

My pulse spikes when his lips curl and he closes the distance between us. He places his hand on my lower back, reeling me toward him. Our bodies touch. The heat coming from him is almost burning me. "You should be afraid."

"I can safely say that I've seen worse. Much worse."

"I hate that you did." He peppers kisses on my forehead, then my cheek, and finally my neck. "If I could, I would put you in a crystal case and keep you safe forever."

His mouth hovers over mine. "You don't know how much it breaks me to put you in danger."

"I was scared," I confess, trembling, and I don't know if it's the memories or being in his arms. I want him so much.

I want him to erase the day, the memories, the horror of not knowing if he'd come out of that hell alive.

202 • CLAUDIA BURGOA

"I've never been more scared of anything in my entire life," he confesses.

"Why?"

"Because even though I can't have you, I would hate to lose you." He leans in, his mouth meeting and parting mine.

It's a kiss filled with longing. I want to tell him that if he really wanted me, I would be his forever.

"We," he says, almost panting.

"Please don't stop. I need you. I need you to remind me that I'm alive, that you're with me, that nothing happened."

He sweeps me into his arms, carrying me upstairs and making his way into the first bedroom. When he sets me back on the floor, he says, "I want you."

He cups my face, kissing me deeper. My arms link around his neck. This kiss is different from anything we've ever experienced. He's taking my pain while giving me his. We're two broken people, and this time, while I try to put him together, he's doing the same with me.

One moment we're kissing. The next, we're undressing each other.

"Teddy." He suddenly stops when we're completely naked. The rawness in his eyes when he talks to me destroys me.

I'm obliterated.

He's going to stop this, us.

I can't deal with another rejection.

Not today—not after everything that's happened between us.

"This thing between us... I wish I could give you what you deserve and more."

The words confuse me. "What does that mean?"

"I can't offer you a lifetime when my job is risky." His hands cup my jaw. His eyes are a mixture of hunger, fear, and distress.

"What if I don't ask you for anything but to make it better today, to make me forget?" I pause, licking my lips. "Just today."

He doesn't respond, just kisses me softly, so softly I feel like glass that might shatter. The touch of his fingertips against my bare skin is gentle, loving. This time there's no urgency or desperation. Carefully, he sets me in the middle of the bed, and our mouths remain together. Seth isn't this gentle. Well, unless I count our first time and the month he spent with me in Chicago after Archer died.

He moves his mouth down my neck to my torso until he takes my breast in his mouth, sucking on it gently. A moan escapes me as I twist in pleasure. He slips his hand between my legs as he continues suckling my other breast.

Heat shoots from his fingertips, making me quiver. This is one of his favorite things to do with me. Lick me, nibble me, and play me with his fingers. My pussy is his preferred body part. He loves to make me come as many times as he can until I beg him to stop. We could go on all day and all night to see who wants to give in first.

But today it's not a game.

I need him inside me, filling me and making me feel alive. Burning so hot that his heart and mine melt into one.

"Stop torturing me," I say before he really even starts to play the game.

His gaze lifts. Those gray eyes stare at me for a few beats. "What do you want?"

"Just you," I say, almost breathless. "No games, no words, and most of all, no regrets. I want you bare without the usual barriers and the shields you put between us."

"Teddy."

"Give me that much. I deserve it. Didn't you just say that you wish you could give me what I deserved?"

"That's not what I said, but it is what I meant."

"Then do it for tonight."

Narrowing his eyes, he sets his forehead against mine. "Theodora," he growls my name.

I'll never understand why my full name sounds more endearing coming from his mouth than calling me Teddy. It's just different or maybe special since he's all mine. He bends, kissing me. Our tongues connecting. I don't know if he's going to stop us, but I pray that he doesn't. Not today.

"Please," I beg one more time.

"You know I'll always give you everything you want."

He kneels at the center of my legs, spreading them apart. Grabbing the base of his thick, long cock, he thrusts it inside me. He stretches me, and I welcome the feel of his dick as he drives in deeper and deeper. My pussy squeezes around his hardness. His eyes lock with mine. They're dark like a night in the middle of a storm.

"Kiss me," I say, and I don't have to beg this time. He tangles his fingers in my hair as he kisses me.

The way he takes my mouth, it's as if he's out of oxygen, and I'm the only person who can keep him alive. We drive against each other. He's pulling out and pushing deeper. Thrusting as hard as he can, trying to become one with me.

I'm fueling the fire inside his body.

He's calming the chaos in my head.

He's putting me together.

He's falling apart.

We're heaven and hell.

And I just want to burst into a million pieces and fuse with him.

I'm close. So close.

His muscles strain as I shake and twist beneath him. He thrashes, pumping faster and harder. We're flying high, and at this moment, no one can touch us. No one can pull us apart, not even him.

When I start coming down from the high, I feel sleepy, and that's when he says, "This might never get easier, but maybe we can find a way."

I don't know what he means, but I close my eyes and fall into a deep sleep.

Chapter Thirty-Four

Seth

TEDDY FALLS asleep after the first time we make love. Any other time, I would hold her until she wakes up. One time with her is never enough, but it has to be for now.

She has to rest since tomorrow will be another stressful day. I text Beacon asking him to call me when he has time. I want to go through his findings. However, it's Grace who calls me.

"Hey," I greet her. "Enjoying your honeymoon? Nothing

says, 'I love you, let's start a new life,' better than chasing bad guys and protecting your brother."

She laughs. "How are you, little brother? I heard you terminated an entire flock of bad men and then got amnesia. That or you have a guardian angel."

"You joke, but that would be ideal." I rub my chin. "Well, the part where I eliminated everyone on my own and then forgot it ever happened. About the guardian angel... It's unsettling to know that someone out there is ahead of us. It's not that I don't like to have competition, I just like to know who's coming to my playground. Have they found anything yet?"

"Nope. Nathan thinks it might take him a few days to find out any information." She clears her throat. "'Only if there's something to find out.' His words."

Grace loves to imitate voices but always does a poor job. I pace back and forth. "This is unsettling."

"Being with Teddy, or not knowing if you have a new friend?"

I walk toward the window, staring at the street. Her question is unexpected, but both things have been on my mind.

"She shouldn't be here." I rub my temples with my thumb and middle finger, closing my eyes briefly. "This is unsafe. We should've sent her with Mom and our grandparents."

"You've worked with civilians before. What makes it different?" I don't like that she's asking questions, trying to... What is she trying to do?

"I don't like working with civilians," I argue.

"You never protest. Why is this different?" She switches the question.

"Please don't make me say it."

"But it'd be great if you finally let the words out. I never realized how much you *care* about her until Nathan explained the issue—with graphics." Her taunting voice is upsetting and sounds like sweet vengeance for all the hard times I've given her since we were children.

"Did he really make graphics?"

"Of course he did, even pulled out old pictures and footage. The way you stare at her, as if she's the only person in this world… The presentation he gave us was an enlightening experience," she assures me.

"That's ridiculous. He wouldn't do that." I think. My little brother has too much time on his hands, and sometimes he wastes it on the most ridiculous things.

"Anyone who knows Nathan would agree that our baby brother is ridiculous. Now, tell your favorite sister what's happening. You need someone to talk to about the events that have transpired in the past week. Knowing you, you won't call the therapist because 'this isn't part of the operation.'" She poorly imitates my voice when she says the last few words.

I can't help but laugh.

"Seth, I'm serious."

"There's nothing to say."

"You care for her? Is that it?"

"I do."

"That's not the entire truth. You more than care for her. You just don't want to admit it to yourself or anyone."

"Maybe."

"Can you give us a little more emotion here? I feel like the *L* word should be spoken."

"No!"

"That sounded like a yes, but I'll deny it under duress."

"I can't love her."

"Well, at least you dare to say the word. Now, explain to me why you *can't* love her."

Why is she stubborn and obtuse? I want to hang up the phone and ignore every emotion that Teddy stirs inside me. Instead of listening to logic and reasoning, I continue the conversation. "Look at my life. I'm always traveling. I just put her in danger."

"This mess wasn't your fault. Your ex was a piece of work."

"If I had taken care of the—"

"Let me stop you there before you go down the hellhole of guilt that you do most of the time. You weren't the one in charge of the cleanup after the initial operation was compromised. You went with the A team to help them. *The fucking A team* was in charge of cleaning up, and they did their best."

"Yes, but—"

"The fucking A team," she repeats as if I don't comprehend what she's saying. "That means our father and our uncles. The guys who've been doing this job for years. The founders of The Organization. This isn't on you, and it's not on them. Some of the people from the cartel flew the coop, and that's not on anyone. Do you understand?"

"I am trying to wrap my head around it, but it's impossible."

"More so when you still blame yourself for the death of

your best friend," she adds, and I hear the snap of fingers. "Which brings us to you avoiding Teddy because of what you think you did to her brother."

"It should've been me."

"Then I would be the broken girl who can't get over her brother's death, and Teddy would be missing you the way Piper misses Archer. It's the same game with different players. You saved our mother from the grief of losing another child. Look at what you did accomplish, not what you think was a failure."

"I try, but it's too fucking hard."

"If this tactic isn't working, you should switch it. Also, give yourself a chance to be with Teddy. She's good for you."

"My job—"

"It's like many others, just a little riskier when there are missions."

"How can you handle things when Beacon is on a mission?"

"I'm with him, but the main thing is that we trust each other. Just like Mom trusts Dad. Does she hate when we go out on missions? So much, but she also understands why we do it and supports us. Maybe after this is over, Teddy will understand more of what you do and still love you with all your flaws. She'll love you the way you love her, but only if you start wooing her instead of being a jackass."

And she's right. All these years, I've been pushing my feelings aside. I've been in love with Teddy for a very long time. Even before we were in Vegas. I just push everything to the back of my mind and keep it away from my heart.

I do love her. All I can say to Grace is, "I do, you know?"

"Yes, but maybe you should say it out loud and act on it."

"If I do, she's the one who'll hear it first."

"You're one of the bravest people I know. Use that courage to be happy too."

She says it as if it's easy, as if I deserve Teddy and her heart. But I can't see it. Maybe when this is over, when it's done, I can finally take a breather.

"Thank you for this talk."

"But are you going to listen to me?"

"I'll try, okay?"

"I love you, but you're just as stubborn as our father."

I snort. "That's impossible."

"Uh-huh. By the way, Nate ran the names of the people you gave him."

"Which people?"

"Sky and Porter Kendrick."

"And?"

"Porter was our grandparents' foster child," she whispers.

"What? And they blacklisted him? Why?"

"I think he's the guy who abused Mom when she was young," she whispers.

"Why would you think that?"

"He was famous, lived with our grandparents… it could be him."

"Do you think he's James's dad?"

"What do you mean James's dad? Isn't our father—"

"No." I tell her about my conversation with Dad.

We're both silent for a few seconds before she says, "I think we should confront them when this is over."

"What's the point?"

"We're adults. Maybe it's time to stop keeping secrets from us. We can handle them."

"Let's get out of this mess alive, and then we can talk about this turn of events, okay?"

"Fine. I'll stay quiet, but only if you promise to call a therapist."

"You're relentless."

"Because I love you. Stay safe, okay?"

"You too. Talk to you soon."

I stare at my phone for several seconds and text Nate, asking to rush the search for the missing link. Those people who have a vendetta against the cartel might be ready to terminate me after we finish the job.

Chapter Thirty-Five

Seth

THE CONVERSATION with my sister stays with me for the next couple of hours. My fucked-up relationship with Teddy. Mom's past. The A team making mistakes and getting past the consequences. They're good at what they do, and because of them, The Organization and the world are better. Still, I don't think I'll ever fill Dad's shoes.

What if I quit and dedicate my life to my business?

I almost cringe at the mere thought of not doing one of the

things I'm most passionate about. Admitting that Beacon was right is painful. The problem is that I don't trust myself.

My mind races with so many thoughts. Around five, I convince myself that there's no point in thinking about my future when I have to concentrate on the now. I begin to prepare dinner. Hopefully, the aroma will wake Teddy, but if not, I'll do it myself. So much for keeping my dick in my pants.

But how could I when she needed me as much as I needed her?

I always need her.

I do because she's a part of me, or maybe I'm a part of her.

That's the problem with us. We're one, and we have to function like two separate entities.

Do I love her?

More than anything in the world, even when she drives me insane. Even when I don't deserve someone as pure as her. I love her.

Making things work between us will be a challenge. I run both hands through my hair. I have to learn to forgive myself for what happened to Archer. And what happened to Piper. Not knowing where she is and if she's okay, it's killing me.

If I could, I would go and look for her, but she would want me to finish this. Before I reach for my phone to check if there's any news about my cousin, I hear Teddy's voice. "I need a gun."

The fuck? I mouth. The muscles on my back tense.

I slowly turn around, finding a freshly awakened Teddy wearing nothing but my t-shirt and rumpled hair. She looks gorgeous, and all I want is to drag her back to bed and fuck her a few more times before we have to leave. I would if she hadn't requested… a gun.

"Did you sleep well?" I ask, pretending she didn't make a ridiculous request.

"A gun," she repeats. "You have to provide me with one."

No. I don't. Where did she get that crazy idea? Telling her no without an explanation will only upset her. I swallow, trying my best negotiating tactics. "I would if you knew how to use it."

She lifts her chin. "I do."

I turn off the stove, cross my arms, and lean my hip against the kitchen counter. This is going to take longer than I expected. I just have to keep this as a friendly discussion before it escalates to an argument and then a fight.

"When was the last time you went to the range to practice?"

She opens her mouth and closes it.

"Just because you did it once—"

"Archer used to take me to practice," she interrupts me, and I don't miss the snark in her tone.

I almost growl. Of course it was him. Why am I not surprised? He always dragged Teddy along with him, treating her like one of the boys. It's not wrong, but he could've been more cautious about what his little sister learned.

There has to be a way around this so that I don't have to give her a gun. "We'd have to go to the range to practice before I give you anything."

"Then let's go."

My eyes glance at her beautiful body. "Not like that."

She huffs. "I'll change, but we have to go. You promised to give me a plan or a way to defend myself if anything happens."

That's not what I agreed to, but she's right. Instead of thinking about my future or us, I should've traced a plan.

"Why don't we eat, and after that, we can plan and maybe find the nearest range?"

She glares at me, skeptical, and sighs. "As long as you don't go back on your word."

"I never do."

"That's right. You never make promises. God forbid you commit to anything."

Where did she get the idea that I don't commit? That is not the point. Maybe the best way to show her a gun is a bad idea is by taking her to the range.

"So what now?" Teddy sips from the bottle of water I brought for her.

We're heading back to the safe house. The shooting range was a big failure. Archer taught her how to use a small hand-gun. The ones I have with me are too big, and each time she shoots, she loses her equilibrium. That's more dangerous than her not being armed.

"We can ask Beacon to give us a bodyguard."

"Aren't they covering us?"

"They are, which is why I don't understand why you need a backup plan."

"You had a bodyguard covering us when they attacked Piper and me."

"He was a guy from another division. They're trained to

guard you against paparazzi and stalkers. Not trained assassins."

She sighs. "You know, when I read my horoscope at the beginning of the month, I thought 'be prepared for new adventures' meant something like, I'd be going on a safari. Which I wouldn't do even if my life depended on it. Not... whatever it is that's happening to me."

This is so ironic.

Should I tell her this is almost like a safari? We're the ones being hunted, and her life definitely depends on it. I doubt she'll find the humor in my statement, though.

"Why are you smirking?"

"I'm not."

"You are. Did I say something funny?"

My phone rings before I can tell her the irony of her statement, and maybe that's for the best.

"Yeah?" I answer the call.

"We got you a gig." Beacon is on the other side of the line.

"Exciting."

"One of Lang's clients has a charity event in San Francisco."

"When?"

"This Saturday."

This doesn't make sense. "Wait, you want me to provide security for the event?"

"No. The plan is to get you an invitation to the Annual Spearman Charity."

"You're putting people in danger."

"HIB provides the security for the event. Instead of using HIB personnel, we'll send people from The Organization."

"Still, there'll be civilians."

"We won't let anyone know you're in San Francisco until that day. It'll take whoever is looking for you several hours before they arrive. We'll release your whereabouts when you're leaving the event."

"What about the people inside?"

"They'll be gone by then. You won't leave the hotel until these men are ready to ambush you."

"Because you'll be the one ambushing them?"

"Exactly."

"I don't love the plan, but we might finish this soon. Let's get this over with."

Chapter Thirty-Six

Seth

ANOTHER BAD IDEA by Beacon Aldridge.

Okay, it's not that bad unless I take into consideration Theodora who's wearing a strapless dress that hugs all her curves and highlights her eyes. It's long, but the slit on the left side, running up her thigh, allows me to look at her tanned legs.

I should give some kind of bonus to Aaron, whose taste in clothes is excellent. They tease the fuck out of me. When this is over, I'll ask her to model each and every little number she's vetoed for this trip.

"Are you sure The Organization will be there?"

"Yes."

"I'm not concerned about me, but all the guests. Can you imagine what would happen if they were to open fire in the middle of the hotel?"

"We have, and there are contingencies for that."

My biggest priority is to keep Teddy safe and ensure that there won't be any casualties. Dad and Beacon have been running scenarios since we agreed to use the gala to not only stop the cartel but also figure out who the friendly fire is.

"Should I learn about the contingency?"

"Security will be tight. Grace is going to be in charge of you if anything were to happen," I explain to her.

"But if we had a plan…" She's a little feistier than usual.

Going to wine country for a couple of days helped distract her, but it wasn't enough. The sex… well, I think that helped plenty. Should we stop and have a quickie in the car before arriving at the gala?

"I don't think I've ever been in the financial district at night," she says. "We could find an alley and…"

She runs her long fingers up and down my leg. "Sex with you is better than a Xanax or a Valium."

"Do you take them often?" I grunt as the tips of her fingers touch my semi-hard cock and jolt as the sound of a car's engine rushing by brings back my attention.

Two vehicles crash against each other in the intersection. I glance at the rearview mirror and a truck speeds toward us.

There's no escape. My shoulders tense as I grip the steering wheel and push the gas, trying to drive along the sidewalk. "Hold on tightly."

Gunfire hails around us. A storm of bullets hits as I'm trying to make my way out of the streets.

"Call Beacon," I order the computer.

"Yep?"

Blood rushes through my ears. This can't be happening. It wasn't part of the plan. If only we had had a team escorting us, I would've had backup. Right now there's not much I can do. "We were ambushed."

"Where are you?"

"Financial district?" I respond as I'm trying to get away.

Once I avoid the collision, I press the gas pedal, running a couple of red lights. I don't know where to go, but the charity is no longer an option. There are two safe houses available. The first thing I have to do is get another vehicle. Scanning the area, I see a barricade ahead of us. A man holding an RPG.

"Beacon, find us. I have to run."

I stop the car, pull Teddy with me, and drag her out of the car. I don't wait for her to walk with me. I have my arm around her waist, and I run fast, hiding behind a car. A ball of fire illuminates the street. There's no time to wait. We run, putting distance between the explosion and us—between the men hunting us and us.

The hissing sound behind us makes me run faster, but we fall when the ground begins to shake.

"If we get separated, run," I tell Teddy. "Run fast, do you understand?"

With the subsequent explosion, I fall down, and everything goes black.

When I wake up, I'm lying on a bed. I push myself up, but a man by the foot of the bed shakes his head. "We'll call the doctor."

"Where is Teddy?"

"Who?" he says, and that's when it hits me.

"Who the fuck are you?"

I've never seen this man in my life.

"It's not important," he says.

"Your boss needs to start paying extra for dragging me out of bed after hours. I was in the middle of a family commitment," the doctor says. He looks at me and begins to check my vitals. He flashes a light. He asks me my name, birthday, and all the questions everyone asks when you have a concussion.

The doctor looks at the man in the room. "Got those questions memorized?"

The guy taps his head. "All of them."

"Good. You can take him and wake him up every two hours. He can't look at screens or do any exercise for the next two weeks." The doctor scribbles something. "I'll send a prescription to the usual pharmacy."

"We need him to help us now, Doc."

The doctor shakes his head. "He might die in the middle of your mission. Tell your boss to choose his battles."

"You're funny, Doctor Spearman. I'll give him the message."

The guy tilts his head toward the door. "It's time to go."

"I'm not going anywhere."

"Then stay, but if they kill your family, we won't be responsible for the massacre."

He is part of the friends… or enemies-of-my-enemy team. I can follow up and then call Beacon. We can get rid of them and the cartel. We'll kill two birds with the same stone.

"About the woman who was with me."

"There was no woman," he answers.

"We got there before they killed you, and the boss ordered me to bring you to the hospital."

"Why do you think I'll cooperate with you?"

"You can leave," he says, leaving the hospital. "I'll even give you money for your Uber."

"What's the catch?"

"Maybe next time we'll let them catch you or kill you."

"We—"

"This is the second time they surprised you. I wouldn't be so sure that your team can take them down on its own." He shrugs. "I could be wrong."

"I need to make a few phone calls."

He shakes his head and opens the door of his truck. He shows me a black hoodie that he gets from the glove compartment. "If you agree to come with me, you must wear this."

I take a step back. Am I still unconscious? "You want me to trust you?"

"Do you have any other option?"

Millions, and none of them involve joining some lunatic who might just kill me after he gets me out of the hospital. "I need to know if Teddy is okay. I don't have time for this."

"The pretty girl who's been with you all along?"

"Yes. That one."

He pulls out his phone. "Did we ever figure out what happened to the little lady who was with him?" He shakes his head and nods. "We're out and trying to come to an agreement. The doc sent you a message. Something about dying. It really doesn't matter."

"Ask about Teddy," I interrupt.

"They don't know where she is, and from what they've heard, neither do your people."

This guy is bluffing. "I have to find her. She's my only priority. If they have her…"

"If they have her, we might be the only ones who can help you before it's too late." He shrugs again as if it's up to me.

My gut tells me to trust him, not sure why, but my father…

Who cares about him? If this is the only way to save Teddy and our families, I have to take a chance.

I snatch the black hoodie. "Fine, but I'll kill you if this is a trap."

He laughs. "We'll see, pretty boy. We'll see."

THE CONTINUATION IS COMING SOON.
SETH AND TEDDY RETURN SOON!

. . .

Continue reading Love After Us >>> here

Their lives are in danger.
And he should let her go.

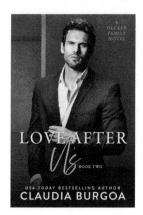

The Organization has one rule.

Never leave any trail behind.

But apparently, I did, and after almost seven years, they came after me.

It wasn't enough that they killed my best friend.

Now they want to kill me.

I owe my best friend my life, and now I put his sister in danger.

I'll do anything to keep her safe, even if it breaks my heart.

Love After Us is a heartstopping, second chance, best friend's little sister love story that you don't want to miss. It is necessary to read After the Vows first.

Do you want to read more about the Deckers?

https://claudiayburgoa.com/wp/decker-family-novels/
Start with Mason Bradley's duet
Suddenly Broken

I'm music royalty.

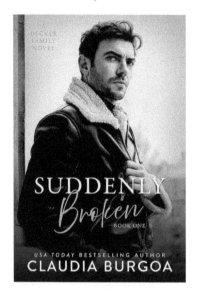

Part of Hollywood's elite.

It's a perk of being the only daughter of Gabe Colt and Chris Decker.

Except, no one knows my fathers are together.

. . .

They kept their marriage private along with their children.

They hid us–and their love for each other–for years.

I grew up sheltered from the celebrity world.

But I was exposed to so many lies…

All I've ever wanted is a normal life.

Friends.

Love.

Sure, I have my brothers and the handsome, geeky Mason Bradley, but that's not enough.

I want more.

I want romantic love.

. . .

Instead of finding it—him–I fell for Porter Kendrick.

I thought he loved me.

He only loved that I worshiped him.

After a loss that rocks my world, I find myself relying on the only friend I've ever had.

The first book in the Unexpected Everlasting duet will invoke tears and heartbreak in a gut-wrenching love story. This book ends on a cliffhanger that'll change everything...

The Unexpected Everlasting Duet is based on Ainsley Decker and Mason Bradley's story. Part of this duet was released as Unsurprisingly Complicated

Claudia is an award-winning, *USA Today* bestselling author.

She writes alluring, thrilling stories about complicated women and the men who take their breaths away. Her books are the perfect blend of steamy and heartfelt, filled with emotional characters and explosive chemistry. Her writing takes readers to new heights, providing a variety of tears, laughs, and shocking moments that leave fans on the edge of their seats.

She lives in Denver, Colorado with her husband, her youngest two children, and three fluffy dogs.

When Claudia is not writing, you can find her reading, knitting, or just hanging out with her family. At nights, she likes to binge watches shows or movies with her equally geeky husband.

To find more about Claudia:
    website

Be sure to sign up for my newsletter where you'll receive news about upcoming releases, sneak previous, and also FREE books from other bestselling authors.

Also By Claudia Burgoa

Be sure to sign up for my newsletter where you'll receive news about upcoming releases, sneak previous, and also FREE books from other bestselling authors.

After the Vows is also available in Audio

The Baker's Creek Billionaire Brothers Series

Loved You Once

A Moment Like You

Defying Our Forever

Call You Mine

As We Are

Yours to Keep

Paradise Bay Billionaire Brothers

My Favorite Night

Faking The Game

Can't Help Love

Along Came You

My Favorite Mistake

The Way of Us

Meant For Me

Finally Found You

Where We Belong

Luna Harbor

Finally You

Perfectly You

Always You

Truly You

Against All Odds: The St. James Family

Until Next Time, Love

Something Like Love

Betting on Love

Accidentally in Love

Waiting for Love

Decker Family Novels

Unexpected Everlasting:

Suddenly Broken

Suddenly Us

Somehow Everlasting:

Almost Strangers

Strangers in Love

Perfect Everlasting:

Who We Are

Who We Love

Us After You

Covert Affair Duet:

After The Vows

Love After Us

The Downfall of Us:

The End of Me

When Forever Finds Us

The Spearman Brothers

Maybe Later

Then He Happened

Once Upon a Holiday

Almost Perfect

Against All Odds Series

Wrong Text, Right Love

Didn't Expect You

Ingram Content Group UK Ltd.
Milton Keynes UK
UKHW010808270323
419227UK00004B/310